D1107388

The Story of

MANON LESCAUT

*"I saw a man elegantly dressed. In spite of his embarrassment, he did
not fail to make a profound bow"*

The Story of
MANON LESCAUT
And the *CHEVALIER DES GRIEUX*

by

The ABBÉ PRÉVOST D'EXILES

Translated from the original text of 1731
by Helen Waddell

Illustrated by Pierre Brissaud

New York · THE HERITAGE PRESS

NOTE BY THE AUTHOR[1]

ALTHOUGH I might have inserted the adventures of the unfortunate Chevalier des Grieux among my Memoirs, it seemed to me that as there was no essential connection between them the Reader might find more satisfaction in seeing them here separately. A tale of this length would have been too long an interruption of the thread of my own story. Far as I am from claiming in that work the quality of an exact writer, I am well aware that a narrative must sometimes rid itself of circumstances that would overweight and cumber it. As Horace advises:

Ut iam nunc dicat iam nunc debentia dici
Pleraque differat ac praesens in tempus omittat.

There is not even need of so grave an authority to prove a truth so simple, for common sense is the original source of this sort of rule. If the Public has found something agreeable and interesting in the history of my life, I dare promise it that it will not be ill satisfied with this addition. It will see in the conduct of M. des Grieux a terrible example of the strength of the passions. I have to paint a blind young man who turns his back on happiness to plunge of his own free will into the worst misfortunes: who with all the qualities that go to form the brightest merit, chooses an obscure and vagabond life in preference to all the

1 The 'Author' to Prévost's first public, was not himself, but the Man of Quality, the late Marquis de * * *. Vol. V has a prefatory notice of his lamented death, and the consequent release of these MSS., so long kept under lock and key by that good gentleman, inasmuch as they related the indiscretions of his acquaintances and not his own, but now edited by his very good friend, Prévost d'Exiles.

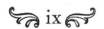

advantages of fortune and of nature: who foresees his misfortunes without wishing to avoid them; who feels them and is overwhelmed by them, without availing himself of the remedies which are continually offered him and which might at any moment put an end to them: in short, an ambiguous character, a mixture of virtues and vices, a perpetual contrast of good sentiments and bad actions. Such is the substance of the picture which I am about to present to the eyes of my readers. Sensible persons do not regard a work of this kind as a useless pastime. Apart from the pleasure of the reading, they will find in it few events that might not tend to the betterment of manners, and in my opinion it is no inconsiderable service to the Public, to instruct it while amusing it.

One is sometimes amazed, reflecting on the precepts of Morality, to see them at once esteemed and neglected, and one asks oneself the reason of this fantastic quality of the human heart, which enjoys ideas of goodness and of perfection and steadily recedes from them in practice. If, for instance, people of a certain order of intelligence and breeding will consider what is the most usual substance of their conversations or even of their solitary reveries, they will readily observe that these turn almost invariably on some consideration of morality. The sweetest moments in life for people of a certain habit of mind are those which they pass either alone, or with a friend, in conversing heart to heart on the charms of virtue, the sweetness of friendship, the means of achieving happiness, the weaknesses of nature that alienate us from it and the remedies that can heal them. Horace and Boileau indicate this kind of talk as one of the finest elements in their image of a happy life. How then does it come that one falls so easily from these high speculations and so soon finds one's self on the level of common men? I am much mistaken if the reason that I am about to give does not explain this contra-

x

NOTE

diction between our ideas and our behaviour: it is that since all the precepts of morality are but vague and general principles, it is very difficult to make a particular application of them to the detail of our morals and our actions. Let us take an example. Souls gently nurtured feel that gentleness and humanity are amiable virtues, and they are moved to practise them: but once at the point of action, they remain often in doubt. Is this indeed the occasion for them? How far is one to go? Is not one deceived as to the object? A hundred similar difficulties hold one back. One fears to become a dupe in one's desire to be a generous benefactor, to show one's self a weakling by seeming too tender and too sensitive: in a word, to exceed or to come short in duties that are too vaguely summed up in the general notion of humanity and gentleness. In this uncertainty, only experience or example can give reasonable direction to the inclination of the heart. Now to give himself experience is not in every man's power: it depends on the various situations in which fortune has placed him. For many, therefore, there remains only example, to serve as guide in the exercise of virtue. It is precisely for this class of reader that works such as the present may be of extreme utility, that is, I would say, when they are written by a person of honour and good sense. Every act described therein is a kind of light, a warning to supply the lack of experience: every adventure is a model on which one may form one's self: it has only to be adjusted to the circumstances in which one finds one's self. The whole work is a treatise of morality agreeably reduced to action.

An austere reader may perhaps take it ill to see me at my advanced age again taking up my pen, to write adventures of love and fortune: but if the observation I have just made is correct, it is my justification: if false, my error will at least be my excuse.

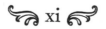 xi

The Story of

MANON LESCAUT

THE STORY OF MANON LESCAUT

Book I

I MUST ask my Reader to hark back to that period of my life when I was to meet for the first time the Chevalier des Grieux. It was five or six months before my departure for Spain. Although I rarely issued from my solitude, my tenderness for my daughter engaged me at times in various trifling journeys, which I cut as short as might be. I was returning one day from Rouen, whither I had gone at her entreaty to plead a suit then pending at the Parliament for the succession to certain estates, to which she had a claim through my maternal grandfather. My road home brought me through Évreux, where I lay the first night; on the day following I arrived in time to sup at Passy, which is five or six leagues distant. To my surprise, I found on entering the Town the inhabitants all commotion, flocking from their houses to crowd round the door of a mean hostelry, before which stood two covered waggons. The horses, still harnessed and smoking with heat and exhaustion, were evidence that the vehicles had but now arrived. I halted a moment to inquire whence all this stir, but got little satisfaction: the crowd was too inquisitive to pay any heed to my questions, and set steadily towards the inn, shouldering its way with a good deal of confusion. Finally, however, an Archer, bandolier and musket on shoulder, appeared in the doorway: I beckoned him towards me, and begged him to tell what all the stir was about. 'Tis naught, Sir, said he, 'tis a dozen *filles de joie* that my company and I are taking to Havre-de-Grâce, to put them aboard ship for America. There are a few pretty ones

 I

among them, and that is what seems to have set these good Souls
all agog. With this account of it I should have gone my way, had I
not been halted by the lamentations of an old woman who came at
that moment out of the inn, wringing her hands and crying that
'twas barbarous, the most pitiful thing and an outrage. And what
may the matter be? said I. Ah Sir, go in, says she, and see if the sight
is not like to break your heart! Curiosity made me dismount from
my horse, which I left with my man. I went in, making my way
with difficulty through the crowd, and saw what indeed was pitiful
enough. Among the twelve girls, chained by the waist six by six,
was one whose face and carriage were so little in accord with her
condition that in any other circumstances I should have taken her
for a Princess. Her grief, the dirt of her linen and of her clothes did
so little to disfigure her that the sight of her filled me with respect
and compassion. She was trying nevertheless to turn away as much
as her chain allowed her, so as to hide her face from the eyes that
beset her: the effort she was making to hide was so natural that it
seemed to come from an innate sweetness and modesty. As the six
guards who escorted this unhappy company were also in the room,
I took their leader aside, and asked if he could throw any light on
the fate of this lovely creature. He could give little, and that of the
vaguest. We took her out of the Hôpital, said he, by order of the
Lieutenant-General of Police. It is not likely that she was put in
there for good behaviour. I have questioned her several times on
the road; she will not answer me a word. But though I have had no
instructions to consider her more than the others, I cannot but have
some regard for her, for she seems to me worth a trifle more than
the rest of them. Yonder is a young man, added the Archer, who
could tell you more about her than I can: he has followed her from
Paris, and hardly for a moment ceased crying. He must be a brother
or a lover. I turned to the corner of the room where the young man
was seated. He seemed sunk in a profound reverie: I have never

seen a more lively image of grief. He was very simply dressed; but the first glance is enough to distinguish a person of birth and breeding. I approached him; he rose to his feet, and I was aware in his eyes, in his face, and in his every gesture, of a spirit so delicate and so noble that I felt instinctively drawn to wish him well. Pray do not let me disturb you, said I, seating myself beside him. But will you be good enough to satisfy my curiosity as to that beautiful creature, who seems to me in no way designed for the sorry condition in which I see her? He made answer courteously that he could not tell me who she was without revealing himself, and that he had strong reasons for wishing to remain unknown. But I can tell you what these wretches are very well aware of, he went on, pointing to the Archers, that I love her with a passion so violent that it makes me the most unfortunate of men. I tried every means in Paris to obtain her liberty; entreaties, stratagem and main force, were alike useless. I then resolved to follow her, should she go to the ends of the earth. I shall embark with her; I shall cross to America. But— and this is the last inhumanity—these dirty rascals, he went on, speaking of the Archers, will not now let me go near her. My plan was to attack them openly a few leagues from Paris. I had four men with me who had pledged me their help for a considerable sum: the traitors left me in the thick of it alone, and made off with my money. To succeed by main force was hopeless; I laid down my arms, and asked the Archers to let me at least follow them, offering to pay them for it: greed of money made them agree. Every time they have given me liberty to speak with my mistress I have had to pay them for it. My purse was soon exhausted, and now that I have not a halfpenny left, they are brutes enough to thrust me back if I take a step towards her. It is only a moment since I ventured to go near her in spite of their threats and they aimed two or three heavy blows at me with the butt of their muskets. And now, to satisfy their greed and get funds to continue my journey even afoot, I

have to sell the poor hack that has so far served me as a mount.

He seemed to tell his tale composedly enough: but a few tears fell from his eyes as he finished it. It seemed to me a most extra-ordinary and most moving story. I do not urge you, said I, to dis-close your secret: but if I can be of use to you in any way, I gladly put myself at your service. Alas! he rejoined, I see no least glimmer of hope: I must submit to the full rigour of my fate. I shall go to America: there I shall at least be free with her I love. I have written to a friend who will have some help ready for me at Havre-de-Grâce. My only difficulty now is how to get myself there: and to provide that poor child, he added, gazing sorrowfully at his mis-tress, with some comforts on the journey. Ah well, said I, I can solve your difficulty: here is a trifling sum which I beg you to accept: I am distressed that I can do you no other service. I gave him four louis d'or without being perceived by the Guards, rightly judging that if they knew that sum upon him, they would sell him their complaisance dear. It indeed came to my mind to bargain with them to let the young lover have constant speech with his mistress as far as Havre. I beckoned the leader to come to me, and laid my proposal before him. In spite of his effrontery, he looked ashamed. It's not, Sir, he answered with some confusion, that we refused to let him speak to the girl, but he wanted to be with her all the time: it puts us out: and it is only fair that he should pay for the incon-venience to us. Come now, said I, let us see how much it would take to keep you from feeling it. He had the audacity to ask two louis. I gave them to him on the spot. But take care, said I, that there is no knavery about this, for I am going to leave my address with this young man so that he can inform me of it, and do you be sure that I have power to have you punished. The whole business cost me six louis d'or. The gracious courtesy and lively gratitude with which the young unknown thanked me confirmed my belief that he was born to rank, and that my liberality was deserved. Before going out

I said a word or two to his mistress. She replied with such charming sweetness and modesty that I could not refrain, as I went out, from a thousand reflections on the incomprehensible character of women.

Once returned to my solitude, I had no way of informing myself of the sequel of this adventure. About two years had passed, and I had completely forgotten it, when chance again brought me in the way of learning the whole story. I had come from London to Calais with my Pupil, the Marquis de . . . We lodged, if I remember rightly, at the *Lion d'Or*, where for various reasons we had to spend the entire day and the following night. Walking through the streets that afternoon, I thought I saw the same young man whose acquaintance I had made at Passy. His clothes were very shabby and he looked much paler than when I first saw him; he was carrying an old portmanteau, as though just arrived in the town. Nevertheless, he was of far too handsome and striking a countenance to fail of easy recognition. I knew him at once. We must, said I to the Marquis, accost this young man. His joy was keen beyond expression when he had in turn recognised me. Ah, Sir, he cried, kissing my hand, so I am permitted once again to express my eternal gratitude! I asked him where he came from. He answered briefly that he had come by sea from Havre-de-Grâce, to which place he had returned from America a short while before. You do not seem to me too much in funds, said I: make your way to the *Lion d'Or* where I am lodging: I shall join you in a moment. I was indeed not long in returning, all impatience to hear the details of his ill fortune and the circumstances of his voyage from America. I used him with the utmost affection, and gave orders in the inn that he should lack for nothing. Nor did he wait for me to urge him to tell me the story of his life. Sir, said he, once we were in my chamber, so nobly have you carried yourself towards me that I should reproach myself with the basest ingratitude if I were to have any reserves from you. I would have you learn not only of my misfortunes and my sorrows, but even my excesses and most shameful weaknesses. I do not think that even while you condemn me you will be able to withhold from me your pity.

I must here warn the Reader that I wrote down his story almost immediately after hearing it, and he may rest assured in consequence that nothing could be more exact or more faithful than this narrative. I say faithful, even to the setting down of the reflections and sentiments which the young Adventurer uttered with all the grace in the world. This then is his story, into which I shall intrude no word that is not his, until it be ended.

I was seventeen years of age, and was finishing my studies in Philosophy at Amiens, where my parents, who come of one of the best families in P***, had sent me. I had led a life so steady and so orderly that my masters held me up as an example to the College. It was not that I made any extraordinary effort to win that distinction, but I have naturally a gentle and tranquil disposition, I was studious by inclination, and they counted to me for virtue what was only an exemption from the grosser vices. My birth, the success of my studies and a few natural good qualities had won me the acquaintance and regard of all the gentlefolk of the town. I came out of my public examination with such general applause that the Bishop, who was present, suggested to me that I should enter the Church, where I could not fail, said he, to win more distinction than in the Order of Malta, for which my family designed me. They already had me wearing the Cross, with the name of the Chevalier des Grieux. The holidays were now at hand, and I was making ready to go back to my father's house, whence he had promised soon to send me to the Academy. My whole regret in quitting Amiens was that I left behind me a friend to whom I had always been tenderly attached. He was a few years older than myself. We had been brought up together, but his family's means being very straitened, he was obliged to take Orders and remain at Amiens behind me, to pursue the

"I stepped forward toward the mistress of my heart. She received the respectful compliments I paid her without seeming embarrassed"

studies becoming to his profession. He had a thousand good qualities: the best of them you will soon recognise in the course of my story, above all an ardour and a generosity in friendship that surpasses the most notable examples of antiquity. Had I but followed his advice, I should have still been good, and still been happy: if I had at least availed myself of his help, in the abyss whither my passions had hurled me, I should have saved something from the shipwreck of my fortune and my reputation: but he has reaped no other harvest from his pains than the grief of seeing them unavailing, and sometimes flung back in his face by a graceless wretch who took offence at them, and treated them as so much pestering.

I had fixed the date of my departure from Amiens. Alas! had I but fixed it one day sooner! I had brought back all my innocence to my father's house. On the eve of the very day on which I thought to quit the town, I had gone for a walk with my friend, who was called Tiberge: we saw the Arras Coach arriving, and followed it out of curiosity to the inn where these coaches stop. We had no other notion than to see who might be in it. A few women came out of it, and at once went their way: but there remained one, a very young girl, waiting alone in the courtyard, whilst an elderly man who seemed to act as escort, was bustling to get her baggage from the rumble. So charming was she, that I who had never given a thought to the difference of the sexes, to whom it had never occurred to look at a girl with a moment's attention, I whose sense and discretion were all men's wonder, I found myself suddenly aflame to the pitch of ecstasy and madness. It was my natural defect to be excessively timid and easily disconcerted: but now, far from being checked by my weakness, I stepped forward towards the mistress of my heart. Although she was even younger than I, she received the respectful compliments I paid her without seeming embarrassed. I asked her what brought her to Amiens, and if she had any acquaintance in the town. She made answer ingenuously that she had been sent here by her family to become a Nun. Love had already so far enlightened me, for all the moment it had held my heart, that I saw their plan the very deathblow to my hopes. I spoke to her in a fashion that made her aware of what I felt, for she was far more experienced than I: it was against her will that she was being sent to the Convent, doubtless to check that bent towards pleasure that had already declared itself, and that was afterwards to be the cause of all her griefs and mine. I combated the cruel intention of her family with all the arguments that awakening love and academic eloquence could bring to my mind. She pretended neither rigour nor disdain. After a moment's silence, she told me that she foresaw only too well that she would be unhappy, but that it seemed to be the will of Heaven, since it had left her no way of escaping it. The sweetness of her gaze, the charming sadness with which the words were spoken, or rather the ascendant of the destiny that swept me to my ruin, suffered me not a moment's weighing of my reply. I assured her that if she was willing to put some trust in my honour and in the infinite tenderness she had already inspired in me, I should consecrate my life to delivering her from the tyranny of her parents, and to making her happy. I have marvelled a thousand times since, thinking on it, whence came of a sudden such boldness and ease in expressing myself: but if it were not Love's way to work miracles, they would never have made him a god. I added a thousand urgencies. My fair unknown was well aware that at my age one is no cheat. She confessed to me that if I could chance on any means to set her free, she would count herself beholden to me for a dearer thing than life. I reiterated that I was ready to attempt anything; but not having sufficient experience to invent any ways of serving her there and then, I stuck at that general assurance, which could be no great help to her. Meantime, her old Argus had come up to us, and my hopes were about to be dashed, but that she had wit enough to supply the barrenness of mine. I was surprised, as her escort joined us, to hear her call me cousin, and tell me without a shadow of embarrassment that since she had been so lucky as to meet me in Amiens, she would put off her admission to the Convent till to-morrow, so as to have the pleasure of supping with me. I entered heartily into the spirit of her ruse: and suggested that she should lodge at an inn where the host, who had set up at Amiens after being long time coachman to my father, was wholly devoted to my service. Thither I myself accompanied her, though the old Escort seemed inclined to grumble a little, and my friend Tiberge who realised nothing of what had passed came after me without uttering a word. He had not heard our talk, but had been sauntering about the courtyard while I spoke love to my beautiful mistress. Dreading his wise judgment as I did, I got rid of him on a pretended errand that I asked him to do for me; so that, once arrived at the inn, I had the delight of conversing alone in the room with the sovereign of my heart. I soon realised that I was less of a child than I had thought. My heart swelled with a thousand delightful sensations of which I had never dreamed: a delicious warmth ran through every vein. I was in a kind of transport which took from me for a time the power of speech, and expressed itself only in my eyes. Mlle. Manon Lescaut, for this she told me was her name, seemed well content with this effect of her charms. She seemed, as I thought, no less moved than I was: she confessed to me that she thought me amiable, and that she would be enchanted to owe me her liberty. She wished to know who I was, and the knowledge increased her affection, for, not being herself of rank though of good enough birth, she was flattered at having made a conquest of such a lover. Together we fell to discussing the ways and means by which she might be mine and I hers. After a vast deal of turning it over, we could think of no other way than that of flight. We should have to cheat the vigilance of her Escort, for though only a servant he was a man to be reckoned with. We arranged that I should order a post-chaise to be made ready that night, and should come back very early in the morning to the inn, before he should be stirring: that we should steal secretly away, and go straight to Paris, and get married as soon as we arrived there. I had about fifty crowns, the harvest of my small savings: she had almost double. We imagined, inexperienced children that we were, that such a sum could never come to an end, and we were equally confident of the success of our other arrangements.

After supping with more enjoyment than I had ever known, I took my leave to carry out our plan. It was the easier to do, as since it had been my intention to go home to my father on the morrow, my scanty baggage was already packed. I had therefore no difficulty in having my trunk carried off, and in bespeaking a chaise for five o'clock in the morning, the time at which the town gates were opened. But I found one obstacle which I had not foreseen, and which came near wrecking my whole designs.

Tiberge, although only three years older than myself, was a youth of ripe judgment and regularity of conduct. He loved me with an extraordinary tenderness. The sight of a girl so lovely as Mlle. Manon, my eagerness to escort her, and the pains I had taken to get rid of him roused him to some suspicion of my love. He had not ventured to come back to the inn where he had left me, lest he should offend me by his return: but he had gone to wait for me at my lodging, and there I found him, although by that time it was nine o'clock. I was annoyed at finding him, and he was quick to see my constraint. I am certain, said he, with no attempt at disguise, that you are meditating some design that you want to hide from me: I see it by your manner. I replied brusquely enough that I was not obliged to give him an account of all my designs. No, he made answer, but you have always treated me as a friend, and that relation supposes a little confidence and openness. He pressed me so long and so close to tell him my secret, that I, who never yet had kept anything from him, at last confided to him the whole story of my passion. He listened with a look of dissatisfaction that made me tremble. Above all, I repented my indiscretion in having acquainted him with the plan of my flight. He told me that he was too utterly my friend not to oppose it with all his might: that he would try to persuade me from it with every argument he could: but that if finally I would not give up my miserable determination, he would warn those who could put a stop to it without fail. Thereon he read me a lecture that lasted more than a quarter of an hour, and wound up by renewing his threat of denouncing me, if I did not give him my word to act with more wisdom and good sense. I was in despair at having betrayed myself so unluckily. However, love having amazingly sharpened my wits in the last two or three hours, I fastened on the thought that I had not told him of my flight being fixed for to-morrow, and determined to deceive him by an equivoque. Tiberge, said I, I have believed up till now that you were my friend, and I wanted to test you by this confession. It is true that I am in love, I have not lied to you: but as far as my flight is concerned, one does not undertake that kind of thing haphazard. Come and call for me to-morrow at nine: I shall take you, if I can, to see my mistress, and you shall judge if she is worth taking such a step for. With a thousand assurances of his affection, he left me alone. I spent the night putting my affairs in order, and towards daybreak I was before Mademoiselle Manon's lodging, where I found her watching for me. She was at her window, which looked out on the street, and catching sight of me, came herself to open the door. We went out without a sound. She had no other baggage to carry than her linen, which I took from her. The chaise was ready to start. We at once left the town behind us. You shall hear later how Tiberge behaved when he discovered that I had deceived him. His zeal was no less ardent. You will see to what extremity he carried it, and what tears I might shed in remembering how ill it was rewarded.

 11

We pressed on with such haste that we reached Saint-Denis before nightfall. I had ridden on horseback beside the chaise, so that we had had little chance to converse unless when changing horses; but when we found ourselves so close to Paris and therefore all but in safety, we took time to refresh ourselves, for we had eaten nothing since leaving Amiens. Passionate as I was for Manon, she knew how to persuade me that she was no less so for me. So reckless were we in our caresses that we had not patience to wait till we should be alone. Innkeepers and Postillions alike gazed at us in wonder, and I could see their amazement at seeing two children of our years in love with one another to madness. Our plans for marriage were forgotten at Saint-Denis. We dispensed with the rights of the Church, and found ourselves Man and Wife without having given it a thought. Assuredly, constant and tender as I am by nature, I had been happy for life, had Manon been faithful. The more I knew her, the more lovable qualities I found in her. Her wit, her heart, her sweetness and her beauty fashioned a chain so strong and so enchanting that I should have counted myself happy never to be free of it. O woeful alteration! That which is ground of my despair might equally have made my blessedness! That very constancy that promised me the fairest of all fates and the most absolute rewards of love is that which has made me the most unfortunate of men.

We took a furnished apartment in Paris. It was in the Rue V..., and, unluckily for me, close to the house of M. de B..., the famous Farmer-General. Three weeks went by, during which I was so absorbed in my passion that I gave little thought to my family and the distress which my disappearance must have caused my father. However, as debauchery had no part in my conduct and as Manon's own behaviour was full of discretion, the tranquillity in which we lived served gradually to recall me to some idea of my duty. I resolved to be reconciled, if it were possible, with my father. My mistress was so lovable that I had no doubt of her power to please him, if I could but find means to acquaint him with her wisdom and merit. In a word, I flattered myself that I could obtain his permission to marry her, for I was now disabused of any hope of being able to do so without his consent. I confided this project to Manon, and impressed upon her that apart from considerations of love and duty, necessity must also have some say in it, as our funds were sadly reduced, and I had begun to retreat from the conviction that they were inexhaustible. Manon received my suggestion coldly. However, as the difficulties she made rose only from her very tenderness for me and her dread of losing me, in case my father, after finding our hiding-place, did not enter into our views, I had not the smallest suspicion of the cruel blow that was about to fall on me. When I urged our necessity, she replied that we still had enough to live on for a few weeks, and that after that she could have recourse to the affection of some relations of hers, living in the Country, to whom she would write. She sweetened her refusal with caresses so tender and so passionate that I who lived only in her, and had no shadow of misgiving, applauded her every argument and every suggestion. I had left to her the keeping of the purse and the paying of our ordinary expenses. Shortly after this I noticed that our table was better, and that she had made some additions to her toilet that were sufficiently costly. As I was well aware that we had hardly more than a dozen or fifteen pistoles left, I showed some amazement at this apparent increase of wealth. She begged me, laughing, to have no concern. Did I not promise you, said she, that I would find resources? I loved her with too much simplicity to be quick to take alarm.

One day I had gone out in the afternoon, and had told her that I should be later coming back than usual. On my return I was surprised to be kept waiting two or three minutes at the door. Our only servant was a little maid about as old as ourselves. On her coming to open the door, I asked her why she had been so long.

She looked confused, and said that she had not heard me knock. I had only knocked once, said I; if you did not hear me, why did you come to let me in? This question so disconcerted her, that not having presence of mind to counter it, she began to cry, assuring me that it was not her fault, and that Madame had forbidden her to open the door until M. de B . . . had gone out by the other staircase, which led from the cabinet. I was so taken aback that I had not strength to go into the apartment. I took the plan of going down again, under pretence of some errand, and I bade the child tell her mistress that I should be back in a moment, but not to let her know that she had spoken to me about M. de B . . .

So great was my consternation that tears came to my eyes as I went down the stairs, without my knowing what sentiment had caused them. I went into the first café, and sitting down at a table, I dropped my head into my hands, to take order with what was passing in my heart. I dared not recall what I had just heard. I would fain have considered it as an illusion, and I was ready, two or three times, to go back to the house without giving any sign of having heeded it. It seemed to me so impossible that Manon could have betrayed me that I was afraid to insult her with the suspicion of it. That I adored her, so much was certain: I had shown her no greater proofs of love than I had from her: how could I accuse her of being less sincere and less constant than myself? What reason could she have for deceiving me? It was only three hours since she had overwhelmed me with her tenderest caresses, and had received mine with ecstasy: I knew my own heart no better than I knew hers. No, no, said I, it is not possible that Manon should betray me! She has not to be told that I only live for her. She knows too well that I adore her. That is no reason for hating me.

Yet M. de B . . .'s visit and his furtive departure were more than I could easily explain. Moreover, I called to mind those trifling purchases which had seemed more than our present means would

᚛ 14 ᚜

warrant. They savoured of the liberality of a new lover. And that confidence of hers in those resources which I knew nothing about; I had some trouble in interpreting all this as favourably as my heart would have me do. On the other hand, she had hardly been out of my sight since we had been in Paris: occupations, walks, entertainments, we had always been side by side: God! one moment's separation would have caused us too much anguish. We must be for ever telling our love; anything else, and we were in mortal distress. I could hardly indeed imagine a single moment in which Manon could have been taken up with another than me. Finally, I thought that I had unravelled the mystery. M. de B . . ., said I to myself, is a man of affairs, and has a wide connection: no doubt Manon's relations have made use of him to hold money in trust for her. Perhaps she has had some from him already, and he came to-day to bring her more. She has played at hiding it from me, to give me a pleasant surprise. Perhaps she would have told me about it if I had gone in as usual, instead of coming here to harry myself. At any rate she will not hide it from me when I speak to her about it myself.

So strongly did I fortify myself with this conviction that it greatly diminished my sadness. I went straight back to our lodging. I kissed Manon with my usual tenderness. She welcomed me lovingly. I was tempted at first to reveal my conjectures, which I now thought of as certain: but refrained, in the hope that she might anticipate me by herself telling me all that had passed. Supper was served. I sat down to table with an air of gaiety; but in the light of the candle that stood between us, I fancied I caught a look of sadness in the eyes of my dear mistress. The thought saddened me also. I observed that her eyes dwelt upon me in other fashion than they were wont. I could not decipher whether it were love or pity: yet it seemed to me it was sweet and wistful. I gazed at her with the same fixedness, and perhaps she in turn found it no easier to judge the state of my heart from my looks. We could neither talk nor eat. At

last I saw tears fall from her lovely eyes: treacherous tears! Ah God! I cried, you weep, my darling, you are grieved enough to weep, and you tell me not a word of your trouble. She did not answer, unless by sighs that did but add to my uneasiness. I got up trembling. I conjured her, with all the instancy of love, to tell me the cause of her tears: I shed some myself, in wiping away hers: I was more dead than alive. A savage would have been softened by the tokens of my suffering and my dread. Meantime, whilst I was thus wholly taken up with her, I heard the sound of several people coming up the stairs. There was a gentle knock at our door. Manon gave me a kiss, and escaping from my arms, passed swiftly into the cabinet, closing the door behind her. I took it that being a little in disarray, she wished to hide from the eyes of the strangers who had knocked. I went to open the door myself. Scarcely had I opened it when I found myself seized by three men whom I recognised at once as my father's lackeys. They did me no violence; but while two of them held me by the arms, the third went through my pockets, and drew from them a little knife, the only steel I had upon me. They asked my pardon for the necessity that made them thus fail in respect; they told me simply that they were acting under my father's orders, and that my elder brother was awaiting me below in a coach. I was so bewildered that I let myself be led without resistance or reply. My brother was indeed awaiting me. I was put into the carriage beside him, and the coachman, who had his instructions, drove us with all speed to Saint-Denis. My brother embraced me tenderly, but spoke not a word, so that I had all the leisure I needed to brood over my ill fortune.

It seemed to me at first so obscure, that I could see no glimmer of light in any least conjecture. I was cruelly betrayed: but by whom? Tiberge was the first to come to my mind. Traitor! said I, it is over with thy life if my suspicions are just. However, I remembered on reflection that he was himself ignorant of my whereabouts, and that no one, therefore, could have learnt them from him. To accuse Manon was an outrage of which my heart was not capable. That extraordinary sadness with which I had seen her overwhelmed, her tears, the tender kiss which she had given me as she fled, seemed indeed an enigma; but I felt driven to explain it as a presentiment of our common misfortune: and at the very moment that I agonised over the accident that had torn me from her, I was credulous enough to imagine her as still more to be pitied than I. The result of my cogitations was to persuade me that I had been recognised in the street by divers acquaintances in Paris, who had then sent the news to my father. This thought brought me comfort. I counted on coming off at the cost of a few reproaches or such chastisement as I must be prepared to undergo from a father's authority. I resolved to submit to it all with patience and to promise whatever was demanded of me, that I might sooner find a way of returning to Paris and bringing back life and joy to my dear Manon.

We arrived in short space at Saint-Denis. My brother, surprised at my silence, bethought him that it was the effect of fear. He undertook to comfort me, assuring me that I had nothing to fear from my father's severity, provided I was disposed to return with docility to my duty and justify the affection which he bore me. He had me spend the night at Saint-Denis, taking the precaution of bidding the three lackeys sleep in my chamber. It caused me sensible pain to find myself in the very inn where I had halted with Manon, on our way from Amiens to Paris. The landlord and the servants recognised me, and were quick to guess at the truth. Ha! I heard the landlord say, 'tis the pretty young Gentleman who came here a month ago, with the little Miss he was so much in love with. Lord, but she was a pretty creature! The poor babes, how they kissed each other! Lord, but 'tis a shame to have separated them! I pretended not to hear anything, and kept out of sight as much as possible. My brother had a two-horse chaise at Saint-Denis, in which

we set out early in the morning, and reached home on the evening
of the following day. He saw my father before I did, to bias him in
my favour by telling how meekly I had let myself be brought home:
so that he received me less sternly than I had expected. He contented himself with a few general reproaches on the fault I had
committed in absenting myself without his leave. As far as my
mistress was concerned, he told me that I had thoroughly deserved
what befell me, for trusting myself to a strange woman: that he had
had a better opinion of my good sense: but that he hoped this little
adventure would leave me wiser. I only took his words in the sense
that agreed with my own ideas. I thanked my father for his kindness in pardoning me, and promised him to be more obedient and
better behaved in future. In my secret heart I was triumphant, for
as things had turned out I had no fear but that I should find opportunity to slip from the house, even before the night was out. We
sat down to supper: I was well teased on my conquest at Amiens,
and my flight with so faithful a mistress. I took the taunts with a
good grace. I was delighted even at the chance it gave me to speak
of that of which my heart was full. But a chance word from my
father caught my ear, and I began listening with breathless attention. He used the word treachery, and spoke of the not disinter-
ested services rendered by M. de B . . . I was stunned at hearing that
name on his lips, and I humbly begged him to explain himself
further. He turned to my brother, asking him if he had not told me
the whole story. My brother answered that I had seemed so quiet
on the way that he did not think I needed that remedy to cure me of
my folly. I could see that my father was hesitating whether to
finish his explanation. I implored him to it with such instancy that
he satisfied me, or rather slew me outright by the cruellest of all
recitals.

He first asked me if I had always been fool enough to believe
that I was loved by my mistress? I told him sturdily that I was sure

of it; that nothing could cause me the least misgiving. Ha! ha! ha!
he shouted, laughing with all his might, this is excellent. You're a
fine dupe, and I like to see you in this way of thinking. It is a great
pity, my poor Chevalier, to send you to the Order of Malta, when
you have the very makings of a patient and obliging husband. He
added a thousand similar jests on what he called my silliness and my
gullibility. At last, as I kept obstinately silent, he went on to say
that so far as he could calculate from the time I had left Amiens,
Manon had loved me for about twelve days: for, he added, I know
that you left Amiens on the 28th of last month; to-day is the 29th of
this one: it is eleven days since Monsieur B . . . wrote to me: I
imagine it would take him eight to come to a perfect understanding
with your mistress: take eleven and eight from the thirty-one days
between the 28th of one month and the 29th of the other, and
you're left with twelve, a trifle more or less. Thereupon the bursts
of laughter broke out afresh. I listened to it all with such agony at
my heart as I feared would not suffer me to sit out this sorry comedy
to the end. You must know, went on my father, since you are unaware of it, that Monsieur B . . . has won the heart of your Princess:
though he tries to make a fool of me, thinking to make me believe
it is pure zeal for my interest that made him wish to take her from
you. Is that the kind of high sentiment you would look for from a
man of his type, who moreover knows nothing about me? He
learned from her that you are my son: and to get rid of the nuisance
of having you about, he writes and tells me your address and the
disorderly way you are living, giving me to understand that it
would take main force to secure you. He offered me his services in
helping to take you by the collar, and it was on information from
him, and from your mistress even, that your brother was able to
catch you napping. So now, congratulate yourself on the lasting-
ness of your triumph! You can conquer quickly enough, Sir Knight:
but you do not know how to keep your conquests.

I could not bear it any longer; every word of it had pierced my heart. I rose from the table, and had only taken a step or two to get out of the room when I fell, senseless and unconscious, on the floor. They brought me quickly round; but when I opened my eyes, it was only to shed a flood of tears, and when I spoke, it was only to utter my piteous grief. My father, who had always a great tenderness for me, strove with all his might to comfort me. I listened, but heard not. I flung myself at his feet: I implored him with clasped hands to let me go back to Paris, to drive a dagger into B . . . It is not true, said I, he has not won Manon's heart: he has done her violence, seduced her by a charm or a potion; perhaps brutally forced her. Manon loves me: do not I know it? He must have threatened her, dagger in hand, to compel her to leave me. What would he not do to ravish so lovely a mistress from me? Oh God! oh God! could it be possible that Manon has betrayed me and ceased to love me! As I harped continually on returning at once to Paris, and was every moment struggling to my feet to do so, my father realised that, in my then state of frenzy, nothing could hold me back. He brought me to a room at the top of the house, and left me there with two men servants to keep me in sight. I was beside myself. To be in Paris for one quarter of an hour, I would have given a thousand lives. I realised that after declaring myself so openly, I would not readily be allowed to leave my chamber. I measured the height of the windows with my eyes. Seeing no possibility of escape that way, I addressed myself ingratiatingly to my two servants. I pledged myself with a thousand oaths to make their fortunes some day, if they would connive at my escape. I urged them, blandished them, threatened them, but again to no purpose. Then I gave up hope. I resolved to die, and flung myself on the bed, determined never to leave it alive. I passed that night and the following day in the same position. The food that was brought me on the morrow, I refused. In the afternoon my father came to see

"I resolved to die, and flung myself on the bed, determined never to leave it alive. I passed that night in the same position"

me. He had the kindness to humour my grief with the gentlest comforting: and laid his commands on me so sweetly to eat something, that I did so out of respect to his orders. Several days passed, during which I ate nothing save in his presence and at his bidding. Every day he urged on me fresh reasons to restore me to common sense, and fill me with scorn for the faithless Manon. It is true that I no longer esteemed her; how could one esteem the most fickle and most treacherous of all creatures? But her image, those enchanting lineaments that I bore deep in my heart, persisted still. I knew myself. I may die, I would say: I ought to die, after so much shame and grief; but I might suffer a thousand deaths before I could forget ungrateful Manon.

My father was surprised to find me still so strongly affected. He knew my standards of honour, and never doubting but that her treachery would make me despise her, he began to think that my constancy arose less from this particular passion than from a general inclination towards women. So convinced did he become, that one day, regardless of anything but his fond affection for me, he came to make me a proposal. Chevalier, said he, I had designed, until now, to have you wear the Cross of Malta: but I see that your inclinations do not lie that way. You like pretty women: I have a good mind to look you out one that will please you. Tell me frankly what you feel about it. I made answer that all women were alike to me now, and that after the misfortune that had just befallen me, I detested them all equally. I shall look out for one, replied my father smiling, who will look like Manon and will be more faithful. Ah, if you have any kindness for me, said I, it is she you must give back to me. Believe me, my dear father, it was never she who betrayed me, she is not capable of such black treachery. It is that false B . . . who is deceiving us, you, and her, and me. If you knew how tender and sincere she is, if you only knew her, you would love her yourself. You are a child, retorted my father. How can you so shut your eyes to what I have told you of her? It was she herself who gave you up to your brother. You ought to forget her very name, and take advantage yourself, if you are wise, of my indulgence towards you. I realised only too clearly that he was right. It was an involuntary impulse that had made me thus take the part of my false love. Alas, I began after a moment's silence, it is only too true that I am the unhappy victim of the blackest of all treacheries. Yes, I went on, with tears of shame, I see too well that I am no more than a child. They had small trouble cheating a gull like me. But I know what I must do to have my revenge. My father would have me tell him my plan. I shall go to Paris, said I: I shall set fire to B . . .'s house, and burn him alive with that false Manon. This outburst made my father laugh, and resulted only in my being guarded still more strictly in my prison.

For six whole months I stayed in it, and for the first of them there was little change in my frame of mind. I had no thought beyond a continual alternation between hate and love, hope and despair, according to the light in which the image of Manon appeared to my mind. Sometimes I saw her only as the most lovable of all girls, and ached with longing to see her again: sometimes I saw only a base and treacherous mistress, and swore a thousand oaths to seek her out only to punish her. I was given books, which served to restore a measure of tranquillity to my soul. I re-read all the Authors I knew. I acquired fresh knowledge. I grew to have an infinite taste for study. You will see how useful I found it in the sequel. The illumination love had given me threw light on many passages in Horace and in Virgil which I had hitherto found obscure. I made a lover's commentary on the fourth book of the Aeneid: some day I mean to publish it, and I flatter myself that the public will find pleasure in it. Alas! I would say as I wrote, it was of a heart such as mine that faithful Dido had need. One day Tiberge came to see me in my prison. I was surprised at the passion with which he embraced me. I had not as yet had any experience of his affection, to think of it as anything more than an ordinary school-boy friendship, such as arises between young folk near in age. I found him so changed and so matured in the five or six months that had passed since I saw him, that his face and the tone of his conversation filled me with a certain respect. He spoke to me rather as a wise counsellor than as a school friend. He lamented the disorders into which I had fallen: congratulated me on my recovery, which he thought well advanced: finally he urged me to profit by this error of youth to open my eyes to the vanity of pleasure. I gazed at him in astonishment. He noticed it. My dear Chevalier, said he, I have said nothing to you but the solid truth, nothing that I have not convinced myself of by serious examination. I was as much inclined as you towards voluptuousness: but Heaven had given me at the same time a taste for virtue. I made use of my reason to compare their several fruits, and I was not long in discovering the difference. The Divine aid reinforced my own reflections. I have conceived for the world an unequalled scorn. Could you guess, he went on, what it is that still holds me in it, that hinders me from fleeing into solitude? Nothing but the tender affection I have for you. I know the excellence of your heart and your mind: there is no good that you could not be capable of. The poison of pleasure has made you lose your way. What a loss to virtue! Your flight from Amiens cost me so much suffering, that I have not had a single happy moment since. Judge for yourself by the steps it made me take. He told me how, after finding that I had tricked him and had fled with my mistress, he took horse to follow me, but as I had had four or five hours' start, he found it impossible to overtake me: yet in spite of that, he arrived at Saint-Denis only half an hour after I had left. Certain as he was that I would stay in Paris, he spent six weeks there, in useless search of me. To every place where there might conceivably be a chance of finding me, there he went, and finally he one day recognised my mistress at the Comédie; her dress was so dazzling that he thought she must owe her fortune to a new lover; he followed her coach to her house, and learned from a man-servant that she was kept at the expense of M. B . . . I did not stop at that, he went on, I came back the next day to find out from her-self what had become of you; as soon as I spoke of you, she broke away from me, and I had to come back to the Country without any further enlightenment. Then I learned what had befallen you, and the terrible distress into which it had plunged you: but I did not wish to see you until I was sure of finding you more at peace.

And so you saw Manon? I answered with a sigh. Alas, you are happier than I, who am doomed never to see her more! He re-proached me for that sigh, as still betokening a weakness for her. He flattered me so adroitly on the goodness of my character and of my inclinations, that from that first visit awoke in me a strong desire to renounce like him all the pleasures of the world, and to enter Holy Orders. Such relish did I find in this idea, that when I found myself alone, I no longer thought of anything else. I called to mind the words of the Bishop of Amiens, who had given me the same advice, and his happy auguries of my future, if I should happen to make that choice. Piety had its share in my considera-tions. I shall lead a simple and Christian life, said I, I shall busy myself with study and with religion, so that I shall have no room to dwell on the dangerous pleasures of love. I shall scorn those things which the bulk of men admire: and as I feel that my heart will only desire what it esteems, I shall have as little to disturb me as to desire. Thereupon I began to picture a way of life that was to be peaceful and solitary. A house remote, with a little wood and a brook of clear water at the foot of the garden: a Library of the Books of my choice: a few upright and sensible friends: a table that would be frugal and temperate, yet elegant. To this, I added an ex-change of letters with a friend who would be living in Paris and would keep me informed on public affairs, less to gratify my curiosity than to divert me with the foolish agitations of men. Shall I not be happy, I concluded; have I a wish that would not be satisfied? It was indeed a prospect that fell in wonderfully with my inclinations; but at the end of all this admirable planning, I knew that my heart still waited: and that if I were to have nothing left to wish for in that enchanting solitude, I must be there with Manon.

Tiberge, however, continued to pay me frequent visits, to confirm me in the design he had inspired: and I took an opportunity to open the subject with my father. He assured me that it was his intention to leave his children free to choose their way of life, and that however I wished to dispose of myself, he reserved only the right to help me by his advice. That which he gave me was of the wisest, and tended less to put me out of conceit with my project than to make me embrace it with better understanding. The re-opening of the Academic year was at hand. I agreed with Tiberge that we should both enter the Seminary at Saint-Sulpice, he to complete his studies in Theology, I to begin mine. The Bishop of the Diocese well knew his worth, and bestowed on him an important benefice, before our departure.

My father, believing me wholly recovered from my passion, put no difficulty in the way of my going. The Clerical habit took the place of the Cross of Malta, the name of the Abbé des Grieux that of the Chevalier. I bent myself to study with such earnestness, that in a few months I had made extraordinary progress. Part of the night was spent upon it, and I lost not a moment of the day. Such was my reputation that I was already congratulated on the dignities I could not fail to win; and though I had never asked it, my name was enrolled on the list for benefices. Nor yet was piety neglected: I was ardent in all its exercises. Tiberge was charmed with what he regarded as his own handiwork, and more than once I saw him shed tears in his happiness over what he called my conversion. That human resolutions are liable to change has never been a matter of surprise to me: one passion gives them birth, another can destroy them. But when I think on the sacredness of the resolves that brought me to Saint-Sulpice, and on the inward joy which Heaven granted me to feel in carrying them out, I am terrified at the ease with which I broke them. If it is true that succour from on high is at any moment as powerful as human passion, let some one explain to me by what fatal ascendancy one finds oneself swept in a moment far from one's duty, without being capable of the slightest resistance, without being sensible of the faintest remorse. I thought myself absolutely purged from the weaknesses of love. It seemed to me that I would prefer a page of St. Augustine or a quarter of an hour of religious meditation, to all the pleasures of the senses, even, I say, those that could be offered me by Manon. Yet one fatal moment hurled me again over the precipice, and my fall was the more irreparable, in that at one plunge I found myself again in the depths from which I had climbed, so that the fresh disorders into which I fell carried me still further towards the bottom of the abyss.

I had passed almost a year in Paris without trying to learn anything of Manon's affairs. It had cost me a good deal at first to do myself this violence, but the ever-present counsels of Tiberge and my own reflections had won me the victory. The last months had flowed by in such tranquillity that I believed myself on the point of forgetting to eternity that charming and faithless creature. The time arrived for my public disputation in the School of Theology: I had asked several persons of distinction to honour me with their presence. My name was thus bruited about in every quarter of Paris. It even reached the ears of my false one. She could not be sure of it, disguised as the Abbé; but some flicker of curiosity or perhaps some remorse at having betrayed me (I have never been able to disentangle which sentiment it was) roused her interest in a name so like my own; she came to the Sorbonne with several other

Ladies. She was present at my declamation, and doubtless had small difficulty in recognising me. I was completely unaware of her presence. There are in these places, as you know, special galleries for Ladies, where they are hidden from view behind a lattice. I returned to Saint-Sulpice, covered with glory and laden with compliments. It was six o'clock in the evening. A moment after my return, they came to tell me that a Lady was asking to see me. I went at once to the parlour. Oh God, what an apparition! There I found Manon. It was she, but lovelier, more dazzling than I had ever seen her. She was in her eighteenth year. Her charms passed all description: an air so delicate, so sweet, so winsome, love's very self. Her whole face seemed to me one enchantment.

I stood dazed at sight of her, and, unable to guess the meaning of her visit, I waited with downcast eyes and trembling, till she should explain herself. Her own embarrassment was for some time equal to mine, but, seeing that my silence persisted, she put her hand over her eyes to hide her tears. Timidly she told me that she knew her faithlessness deserved my hate, but that if I had really ever had any tenderness for her, there had been a good deal of hardness on my side in letting two years go by without ever trying to find out what had become of her, and far more now in seeing the state she was in in my presence, and never saying a word to her. The upheaval in my soul as I listened was beyond expression. She sat down, I remained standing, half turned away, not daring to look at her directly. Several times I began to reply, and had not the power to finish. At last, with an effort, I uttered one anguished cry, False Manon! Ah, False! False! Again she said, weeping hot tears, that she did not mean to justify her falseness. What do you mean then? I cried. I mean to die, said she, if you do not give me your heart again, for I cannot live without it. Then ask my life, false love! I answered, with tears that I tried vainly to restrain, ask my life, it is all that is left me to give you, for my heart has never ceased to be yours. Scarcely had I uttered the last words than she rose in an ecstasy and came to clasp me in her arms. She overwhelmed me with a thousand passionate caresses. She called me by all the names that love can find for its most eager tendernesses. As yet I made but languid response. What a transition, in very truth, from the peace which had surrounded me to the stormy emotions which I felt awakening! I was aghast. I was shivering as when one finds one's self at night in a desolate countryside: one feels one's self transported into a new order of things: one is seized by a secret horror, that only abates after long considering one's surroundings.

We sat down side by side. I took her hands in mine. Ah Manon! said I, gazing at her with sad eyes, I had not a thought of the black treachery with which you repaid my love. It was easy for you to deceive a heart of which you were absolute sovereign, and whose whole happiness was set in pleasing and obeying you. Tell me, have you found any since as tender and as submissive? No, no. Nature will hardly have made another of the same temper. Tell me at least if you have sometimes regretted it? What am I to count on in this return of tenderness that brings you here to-day to comfort me? I see only too well that you are lovelier than ever: but in the name of all the grief that I have suffered for you, tell me, lovely Manon, if you will be more faithful?

She made answer, telling me such touching things of her repentance, and bound herself to constancy with so many vows and protestations, that she softened me beyond telling. Dearest Manon, I cried, profanely mingling the language of passion and Theology, you are too adorable for a created thing. I feel my heart swept by a conquering delight. All that they say at Saint-Sulpice about free will is a Chimæra. I am to lose my fortune and my name for you, that I foresee, I read my destiny in your lovely eyes: but is there any loss for which your love would not console me? The favours of fortune move me not at all: fame seems to me a wreath of smoke:

all my plans for holy living were vain imaginings. Whatever good may be in life, apart from what you bring me, is contemptible, since not for a moment could it steel my heart against a single glance from your eyes. Yet, even as I promised her a general oblivion of her faults, I wished to learn from her how it was she had suffered herself to be seduced by B . . . She told me that he had seen her at her window, and had fallen violently in love with her: that he had declared himself as a Farmer-General would, by stating in a letter that payment would be proportionate to favours received: that she had capitulated, yet at first with no other design than to get sufficient money out of him to keep us in comfort, but that then he had dazzled her with such magnificent promises that she had, little by little, been shaken: that I might gauge her remorse by the grief she had shown on the eve of our separation: that in spite of the luxury in which he had kept her, she had never known happiness with him, not only because she found nothing in him, said she, of my own delicacy of feeling or charm of manner, but because in the very midst of the pleasures with which he was for ever plying her, her heart mourned in secret over the memory of my love and her own faithlessness. She spoke to me of Tiberge, and the extreme agitation which his visit had caused her. A sword thrust at my heart, she went on, would have shaken me less. I turned my back on him, for I could not bear his presence for a moment. She went on to tell me how she had come to learn of my stay in Paris, of the change in my way of life, and my examination in the Sorbonne. She assured me that she had been in such agitation during the disputation that she could hardly restrain not only her tears, but even her sobs and cries, which had more than once all but broken out. Finally she told me that she had been last in quitting the hall, so as to hide her disorder, and that, following only the impulse of her heart and the eagerness of her desires, she had come straight to the Seminary, determined to die there if I would not forgive her.

Where is the barbarian who would not have been touched by repentance so keen and so tender? For my part, I felt at that moment that for Manon I would have sacrificed every Bishopric in Christendom. I asked her what new disposition she thought best in our affairs. She said that we must at once leave the Seminary, and put off making our plans till we were in a safer place. I agreed to all her wishes without a demur. She entered her carriage and drove off to wait for me at the corner of the street. A moment later, I made my escape, without the porter seeing me. I got in beside her. We drove to the tailor's. Once again I put on spurs and sword. Manon paid; I had not a penny, for fearing that I might meet some obstacle to my escape from Saint-Sulpice, she had been unwilling to let me go back for a moment to my room to get my money. For that matter, my store of it was small, and she rich enough, thanks to B . . .'s liberality, to set little by it. Even at the tailor's we began planning what our next steps should be. To convince me how completely she was sacrificing B . . . to me, she was determined to consider him in nothing. I am going to leave him his furniture, said she, for it belongs to him: but I shall take away—'tis only justice—the jewels and the sixty thousand francs that I have got out of him in the last two years. I have given him no power over me, she added, so we need not be afraid to stay in Paris, and we shall take a comfortable house where we can live and be happy together. I pointed out to her that if there were no risk for her, there was a good deal for me, since I was bound sooner or later to be recognised, and should be in constant danger of the same mishap I had already had experience of. She let me see that she would grieve at quitting Paris. So much did I fear to vex her that there was no risk I would not have despised to please her. However, we found a reasonable compromise, which was to rent a house in some village in the outskirts of Paris, whence it would be easy for us to come to town when pleasure or business called us thither. We fixed on

Chaillot, which is within easy distance. Manon went straight back to her house, I went to wait for her at the little gate of the Jardin des Tuileries. An hour later, she arrived in a hackney coach with her maid, and several trunks in which her clothes and whatever valuables she had were packed.

We were not long in reaching Chaillot. The first night we lodged at the inn, so as to have time to look about for a house, or at any rate a convenient apartment. The day after, we found one to our taste. My happiness seemed to me then secure beyond all shaking. Manon was sweetness and indulgence itself. The tendernesses with which she encompassed me were so exquisite that I felt myself far overpaid for all my pain. Both of us had learned a little from experience, and so we took counsel with each other as to the stability of our fortune. Sixty thousand francs, which was the substance of our wealth, was not a sum that could be stretched to cover the course of a long life. Nor were we, moreover, inclined to live too straitened. Manon's prime virtue was not, any more than my own, economy. This then was the plan I proposed. Sixty thousand francs, said I, can keep us for ten years. Two thousand crowns will be enough for each year, if we go on living at Chaillot. We shall live like gentlefolk, but simply. Our only expenses will be the keeping of a carriage, and going to plays and the like in Paris. We shall take order with ourselves. You like opera: we shall go three times a week. As for cards, we shall limit ourselves never to lose more than ten pistoles. In ten years' time there is bound to be some change in my family: my father is elderly, he might die. I shall fall into some property, and then we shall be secure from all our other fears. This arrangement would not have been the most foolish action of my life, if only we had had sense enough to abide by it. But our resolutions hardly saw the month out. Manon was mad for pleasure; so was I, for her. Every moment brought new occasions for spending: and far from grudging the sums that she lavished, sometimes to profusion, I was the first to buy her whatever I thought would please her. Even our continuing to live at Chaillot began to fret her. Winter drew near: everyone was going back to town, and the country deserted. She proposed that we should take up house again in Paris. I would not consent to that; but to meet her wishes I said that we could rent a furnished apartment and spend the night there whenever we were too late leaving the assembly, to which we went several times a week: the inconvenience of coming back so late to Chaillot was the excuse she gave for wishing to leave it. We thus set up two establishments, one in town, one in the country. It was this change that put the finishing touch of confusion to our affairs, in bringing about two happenings that resulted in our ruin.

Manon had a brother in the Life Guards. Unluckily, his lodging in Paris happened to be in the same street as our own. One morning he recognised his sister, having caught sight of her at a window, and came straight to our house. He was a brutal fellow, and with no sense of honour. He came into our room, swearing horribly: and as he knew something of his sister's past, overwhelmed her with insults and reproaches. I had gone out the moment before, which was undoubtedly lucky either for him or for me, who was in no way given to submit to insult. I only came back to the house after he had gone. Manon's dejection made me certain that something out of the ordinary had occurred. She told me of the distressing scene she had just come through, and the brutal threats of her brother. So fierce was my resentment that I would have gone off there and then to avenge her had she not stayed me by her tears. Whilst I was still talking it over with her, the Guardsman re-entered the room where we were, unannounced. I should not have received him as civilly as I did if I had known who it was: but, after a gay greeting to us both, he had time to say to Manon that he had come back to apologise for his fit of rage: that he had thought her to be living a disorderly life, and this had kindled his wrath; but that he had found out who I was

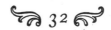

from one of our servants, and been given such a good report of me that he would fain be on friendly terms with us. Although the idea of this information coming to him from one of my lackeys had something bizarre and revolting about it, I received his civilities with courtesy. I thought it would please Manon. She seemed charmed to find him bent on a reconciliation. We kept him for dinner. In a few moments he had made himself so much at home, that on hearing us speak of going back to Chaillot, nothing would do him but he must come too. He must therefore be given a seat in our carriage. It was an act of possession: so agreeable did he find the regular sight of us that he soon made our house his own, and himself master in some sort of all that we had. He called me brother, and under pretext of brother's privilege, put himself on such a footing that he would bring all his friends to our house at Chaillot and entertain them at our expense. He had himself magnificently turned out at our charge, and he even got us to pay all his debts; I closed my eyes to this tyranny, so as not to displease Manon. I pretended even not to notice that he got considerable sums from her from time to time. True, being a great gambler, he had the fairness to pay her back part of them when luck was with him. But our own fortune was too modest to supply for long such reckless expenditure. I was about to explain myself pretty strongly to him and get rid of his importunity, when a fatal accident relieved me of that trouble, while bringing upon us another which engulfed us beyond recovery.

We had spent the day in Paris and stayed over night, as very often happened. The maidservant, who was left to keep house in Chaillot on these occasions, came next morning to tell me that fire had broken out in my house the night before, and that there had been a good deal of difficulty in putting it out. I asked her if the furniture had been damaged. She answered that there had been such confusion, thanks to the crowd of strangers who came to help, that she could answer for nothing. I trembled for our money, which was locked in a little chest. I made my way with all haste to Chaillot. My pains were idle. The chest was gone. I realised then that one can love money, without being a miser. This loss pierced me with such lively anguish that I thought I should go out of my mind. In one flash I saw all the misfortunes that threatened me. Poverty was the least of them. I knew Manon: I had proved only too surely that however faithful and however fond she might be in good fortune, one could not count on her in want. She cared too much for pleasure and plenty to sacrifice them for me. I shall lose her! I cried. Unhappy Chevalier, you are again to lose all that you love! The thought threw me into an agony so frightful that I wondered for a moment if I would not do better to let death put an end to all my sorrows. I had, however, enough sense left to cast about for any possible way out. Heaven brought to my mind an idea that checked my despair. I judged that it might be possible to hide our loss from Manon, and that either by industry or by some stroke of luck I might be able to maintain her well enough to feel no pinch of necessity. I had calculated, said I to myself by way of consolation, that twenty thousand crowns would last us ten years. Suppose the ten years were up, and that none of the changes I had counted on in my family had taken place. What would be my next step? I am not too sure: but whatever I should do then, is there anything to hinder me doing it now? How many people are living in Paris who have neither my wits nor my abilities, and none the less make a living out of such talents as they have? And has not Providence, I went on, meditating on the various conditions of life, has not Providence arranged things with a good deal of wisdom? The Great and the Wealthy are most of them fools: that is plain to anyone who has seen something of the world. Now, in this there is an admirable justice. If they were to add intelligence to their riches, they would be too happy, and the rest of mankind too wretched. To the latter are granted such gifts of body and soul as serve to raise them out of misery and poverty. Some share in the riches of the Great by helping them to their pleasures, they make them their dupes: others aid in their instruction, they try to make decent men of them; it is rare indeed that they succeed therein, but that is not the object of the divine wisdom: they still obtain some fruit of their labours, to live, namely, at the expense of those whom they instruct: and so, however one looks at it, there is a fine source of income for the lesser folk in the folly of the wealthy and the Great.

These thoughts helped me to pluck up heart and wits. I resolved first to consult Manon's brother, M. Lescaut. He knew Paris through and through, and I had had only too many opportunities to realise that it was neither from his own property nor from the King's pay that he drew the best part of his income. All that I had left was a poor score of pistoles, which had luckily been in my pocket. I showed him my purse, explaining my mishap and my fears, and I asked him if there was any choice left me but to die of hunger or blow my brains out in despair. He made answer that only fools blew their brains out: as for dying of hunger, plenty of able people were reduced to that, because they would not use their wits: that it was for me to find out what I was fit for: and that I might be sure of his help and his advice in whatever I undertook. All this is pretty vague, M. Lescaut, said I, my necessities demand a readier remedy: for what would you have me say to Manon? Talking of Manon, he rejoined, what have you to worry about? Haven't you got in her a ready way out of your difficulties whenever you like? A lass like that should be able to keep us all, you, and herself and me. He cut short the retort which this impertinence deserved, by going on to say that he would guarantee a thousand crowns to share round before night, if I would take his advice: that he knew a Nobleman so free-handed in his pleasures that he was sure he would never grudge a thousand crowns to spend a night with such a lass as Manon. I stopped him. I had thought better of you, said I, I took it that the motive you had in giving me your friendship was a feeling for your sister very different from your present one. He had the impudence to confess to me that he had always been of the same mind, and that her honour once lost, as hers was, he would never have become reconciled with her but for the hope of getting some profit out of her misconduct. It was easy for me to judge how he had duped us. None the less, whatever emotion his words had roused in me, the need I had of his help forced me to answer, with a laugh, that his method was a last resource only to be applied to in extremity. I begged him to suggest some other course. He then proposed that I should turn to account my youth and the good looks that nature had given me to get into the good graces of some ancient and liberal-minded Lady. For this project I had as little relish; it would have meant infidelity to Manon. I suggested cards as the easiest means, and the one most agreeable to my condition. He said that cards were indeed a resource, but one that required management: that to undertake to play with nothing but ordinary luck was the sure way to complete my ruin: that to attempt to use by one's self, and without an ally, the trifling aids which a clever man employs to adjust the inequalities of fortune, was too dangerous: that there was a third way, that of combination: but that my youth made him afraid that the gentlemen who were his confederates might judge me lacking as yet in the qualities proper to their profession. Nevertheless, he promised me his good offices with them, and, what was more than I expected of him, he offered to lend me some money when I should find myself pressed for it. The only favour I asked of him, for the present, was to say nothing to Manon of the loss which I had suffered, or of the subject of our conversation.

I left his lodging, in rather less spirits than I had entered it. I repented even of having trusted him with my secret. He had done nothing for me that I could not have had from him without that confession, and I was mortally afraid that he would betray the promise he had given me to say nothing to Manon. I had reason to fear, moreover, after this revelation of his sentiments, that he might form a plan to get some profit out of her, to quote his own words, by taking her out of my hands, or at least by advising her to leave me and attach herself to some richer and luckier lover. Thereupon I fell prey to a thousand reflections, which only resulted in torturing me and in renewing the despair of the morning. It occurred to me several times to write to my father, and to affect a new conversion so as to obtain from him some monetary aid; but I recalled to mind that in spite of all his kindness he had kept me close prisoner for six months for my first offence: I was very sure that after such a scandal as my flight from Saint-Sulpice must have caused, he would use me with much more rigour. In the end, the confusion of my thoughts produced one which brought peace on the instant to my mind, and left me astonished at not having thought of it sooner. It was to have recourse to my friend Tiberge, in whom I was sure always to find the same depth of ardour and of affection. Nothing is more remarkable and nothing does more honour to goodness than the confidence with which one approaches those whom one knows to be upright; one feels that there is no risk to be run. If they are not always in a position to offer aid, one is sure at least of kindness and compassion. The heart which takes such pains to close itself from other men, opens naturally in their presence, as a flower opens to the light of the sun from which it looks for naught but sweet and useful influences.

It seemed to me that I owed it to the protection of Heaven that the thought of Tiberge had come so aptly to my mind, and I resolved to seek some way of seeing him before the day was over. I returned home at once to write him a brief note and appoint a place suitable to our interview. I urged silence and discretion upon him as one of the most important services he could render me in the state of my affairs. The joy which the hope of seeing him inspired in me effaced the traces of distress which Manon must otherwise have detected in my countenance. I spoke to her of our misfortune at Chaillot as of a trifle which need not alarm her: and as Paris was the place in the world where she most delighted to be, she was not ill pleased to hear me say that it would be convenient to stay there until some trifling damage caused by the fire at Chaillot had been made good. An hour later I received a reply from Tiberge, promising me to be ready at the place appointed. I hastened to it with impatience. I felt some shame none the less in going to meet the eyes of a friend whose very presence was a reproach to my disorders; but the conviction that I had of the goodness of his heart and the thought that it was to Manon's interest, gave me courage to brave it out. I had begged him to come to the garden of the Palais-Royal. He was there before me. He came and embraced me as soon as he caught sight of me. For a long time he held me clasped in his arms, and I felt my face wet with his tears. I told him that I had nothing but confusion in presenting myself to him, and that my heart had a lively sense of my ingratitude; that the first thing which I entreated of him was to let me know if I might still look upon him as my friend, after having so justly deserved to lose his esteem and his affection. He answered me in the tenderest tone that nothing could make him renounce his friendship; that my very misfortunes, and—if I would allow him to say so—my faults and my disorders, did but redouble his tenderness towards me; but that it was a tenderness mingled with the keenest pain such as one feels when one sees the beloved on the verge of ruin without being able to give him aid. We sat down upon a bench. Alas! said I with a sigh that came from the depth of my heart, your compassion must be extraordinary, my dear Tiberge, if you assure me that it is equal to my sufferings. I am ashamed to let you see them, for I confess that the cause of them is nothing to be proud of: but the effect is so unhappy that one need

not love me as much as you do to be softened by it. He asked me as
a proof of friendship to tell him without disguise all that had happened to me since my departure from Saint-Sulpice. I satisfied his
request, and far from dissembling any truth or diminishing my
faults to make them more excusable, I spoke to him of my passion
with all the force with which it inspired me. I represented it to him
as one of those particular strokes of fate when it is set upon the
destruction of its victim, and from which it is as impossible for
virtue to defend itself as for wisdom to foresee them. I painted a
lively picture of my agitations and my fears, the despair in which I
had been two hours before seeing him, and that into which I must
relapse if I were to be abandoned by my friends as pitilessly as by
fortune: in short, I so moved the kindly Tiberge, that I could see
him as much distressed by compassion as I was by the weight of my
own griefs. He did not cease to embrace me and exhort me to take
courage and be comforted: but as he still took it for granted that I
must be separated from Manon, I gave him clearly to understand
that it was this separation which I regarded as the greatest of my
misfortunes, and that I was prepared to suffer not only the last extremity of wretchedness but the most cruel of deaths, rather than
submit to a remedy more intolerable than all my griefs put together. Now then, explain yourself, said he, what sort of help is it
in my power to give you, if you rebel against every suggestion I
make? I could not say to him that it was his purse I had need of: but
in the end he realised it: and, confessing that he thought he under-
stood me, he remained for some time lost in thought, with the air
of a man in doubt. Do not think, he soon continued, that my ab-
straction springs from any coolness of zeal or affection; but to what
alternative have you driven me, when I must either refuse you the
only help you are willing to accept, or wound my sense of right in
granting it; for is it not to share in your misconduct, if I give you
means to persevere in it? And yet, he went on after a moment's re-

flection, I imagine that the clamorous necessity into which poverty has thrown you leaves you no chance to choose the better part; one must have tranquillity of mind to relish wisdom and truth. I shall find means to let you have some money. Permit me, my dear Chevalier, he added, embracing me, to make only one condition, that you will let me know the place of your abode, and that you will suffer me at least to do what I can to bring you back to that goodness which I know you love, and from which only the madness of your passion has led you astray. I granted him frankly whatever he asked, and I prayed him to pity the malignity of my fate which suffered me to profit so little by the advice of so upright a friend. He took me with him to a Banker of his acquaintance, who advanced me a hundred pistoles on his bill: for he had no ready money. I have already said that he was not rich. His benefice was worth two thousand francs, but as this was his first year in possession, he had not yet received any income from it; it was on its future fruits that he made me this advance.

I realised the full cost of his generosity. I was touched by it even to the point of lamenting the blind and fatal love that made me outrage every right. For a few moments virtue had strength enough in my heart to rebel against my passion, and in that one instant of illumination I at any rate saw the shame and the indignity of my chains. Yet the struggle was slight and brief. The sight of Manon would have brought me headlong from heaven, and I was amazed, when I found myself again beside her, that I could have thought shame for a moment of the tenderness that so dear a heart deserved.

Manon was a creature of a most unusual disposition. Never was girl less attached to money than she: but she never knew a moment's peace of mind if there was any fear of lacking it. Pleasure and pastime she must have: she would never have cared to touch a penny if one could amuse one's self for nothing. She never cared to know how much one had, provided she could spend a merry day; so that as she was neither extravagantly fond of cards nor much taken by costly display, nothing was easier than to content her if each day brought forth the diversion that she loved. But to be continuously amused was so necessary to her that failing it one could count not at all on her humour or her inclinations. Although she loved me tenderly, and although I was the only person, as she herself confessed, who could give her the full sweetness of the delights of love, I was almost certain that her tenderness would make no way against certain fears. She would have preferred me to the whole earth, given a modest fortune; yet I never doubted but that she would abandon me for some new B . . . when I should be left with nothing but constancy and fidelity to offer her. I determined therefore so to regulate my personal expenditure that I should always be prepared to supply her own, and to deprive myself of a thousand necessaries rather than limit her even in what was superfluous. The thought of the carriage alarmed me more than all else, for I could see no possibility of being able to keep up a coachman and horses. I opened my difficulty to M. Lescaut. I had not concealed from him that I had received a hundred pistoles from a friend. He again repeated that if I were willing to try my fortune at cards he would not despair, given the cheerful sacrifice of a hundred francs to treat his comrades, of my admission, at his recommendation, into the league of industry. Whatever repugnance I might have for cheating, I let myself be driven by necessity.

M. Lescaut introduced me that same evening as a relative of his own; he added that I was all the likelier to succeed as I was in need of the greatest favours of fortune. However, to make it clear that my poverty was not that of a nobody, he informed them that I was minded to give them a supper. The offer was accepted. I entertained them magnificently. There was much talk of the charm of my appearance and of my natural advantages. It was declared that much might be hoped from me, since, as something in my face

suggested the man of honour, no one would be on guard against my artifices. In short, M. Lescaut was thanked for having procured for the order a novice of my worth, and one of its Knights was entrusted with the task of giving me for a few days the necessary instructions. The principal theatre of my exploits was to be the Hotel Transylvania, where there was a Faro table in one hall, and divers other games of cards and dice in the gallery. This Academy was conducted for the profit of Prince de R . . . who was then living at Clagny, and the greater number of his officers belonged to our association. I was not long in profiting by my master's instructions. I learned above all to be adroit in turning over, in playing the wrong card, and with the help of a pair of deep Ruffles at the wrist, I had sufficient sleight of hand to deceive the eye of the cleverest, and to bring to ruin many an honest player. This unusual skill so hastened the increase of my fortune that I found myself in a few weeks master of considerable sums, besides those which I shared honestly with my associates. I was now no longer afraid to reveal to Manon our loss at Chaillot, and to console her for the distressing news I rented a furnished house, where we established ourselves with every appearance of wealth and security.

Tiberge had not failed meantime to pay me frequent visits. His moralising was interminable. Again and again he started afresh upon the wrong I was doing to my conscience, my honour, and my fortune. I listened to his advice with affection, and although I had not the least inclination to follow it, I gave him credit for his zeal, because I knew the source whence it sprang. Sometimes I teased him pleasantly in Manon's very presence, and exhorted him not to be more scrupulous than a great many Bishops and other Priests, who could contrive very well to make a mistress and a benefice agree. Look, I would say, indicating the eyes of my own mistress, and tell me if there are any faults that cannot be justified by so lovely an occasion as these. He called in patience to his aid, taxed it

"*The principal theatre of my exploits was the Hotel Transylvania, where there was a Faro table in one hall, and divers other games of cards*"

indeed far enough; but when he saw that my riches were increasing, and that not only had I given him back his hundred pistoles, but having rented a new house and doubled my expenses, I was about to plunge deeper than ever into pleasures, a complete change came over his tone and bearing. He complained of my growing hardened; he threatened me with the chastisements of heaven, and prophesied a part of those misfortunes which indeed were not long in befalling me. It cannot be, said he, that the wealth which serves to maintain you in your disorders should have come to you by legitimate channels. You have acquired it unjustly; it will be snatched from you in like manner. The most terrible punishment from God would be to continue you in the tranquil enjoyment of it. All my counsels, he added, have been useless to you; I see only too well that they will soon be vexatious. Farewell, weak and ungrateful friend. May your guilty pleasures vanish like a shadow! May your wealth and your gold perish without redress, and you be left stripped and solitary to realise the vanity of that good which has intoxicated you to madness! It is then that you will find me ready to love you and to serve you; but I break this day every connection with you, and I abhor the life you lead. It was in my own room, under the eyes of Manon, that he made me this Apostolic speech. He got up to go. I would have kept him back, but I was checked by Manon, who said that he was a madman and better let go.

His words did not fail to make some impression on me. I point out thus the various occasions on which my heart felt some returning impulse towards good, because it was to this memory that I finally owed some measure of strength in the greatest misfortunes of my life. Manon's caresses soon dissipated the vexation which this scene had caused me. We continued to lead a life wholly compounded of pleasure and love. The increase of our riches redoubled our affection. Venus and Fortune had no happier or more tender slaves. God! why call the world a place of wretchedness when we can know in it delights so exquisite! But alas! it is their frailty that they pass too soon. What other happiness would one seek, if it was their nature to last for ever? Ours had the common lot, to last but a little while and to be followed by bitter regret. I had won such considerable sums at cards that I began to think of investing part of my money. My servants were not unaware of my successes, especially my own valet and Manon's maid, before whom we often talked without restraint. The girl was pretty, my valet in love with her. They had to do with young and easy-going masters, whom they imagined they could easily hoodwink. They conceived the plan of so doing, and carried it out so disastrously for us that they put us into a position from which we never recovered.

M. Lescaut had invited us to sup with him: it was towards midnight when we came back to the house. I called my valet, Manon her maid: neither appeared. We were told that no one had seen them in the house since eight o'clock, and that they had gone out after seeing to the removal of several boxes, according to orders which they said they had received from me. I had a partial foreboding of the truth, but any suspicions I had were beggared by what I beheld on entering my room. The lock of my cabinet had been forced, and my money stolen, with all my clothes. Even as I stood, turning over what had befallen me, Manon came all alarm to tell me that equal ravages had taken place in her own chamber. The blow seemed to me so cruel that only an extraordinary effort of reason hindered me from an outburst of tears and lamentation. Fear of communicating my despair to Manon made me assume an indifferent countenance. I told her jestingly that I should revenge myself on some dupe at the Hotel Transylvania. However, she seemed so conscious of our disaster that her sadness had more effect in distressing me than my feigned gaiety in restoring her prostration. We are lost! said she, with tears in her eyes. In vain I tried to comfort her by my caresses. My own tears betrayed my despair and my consternation. In truth, we were ruined, so completely that we were left not so much as a shift.

My first step was to send at once for M. Lescaut. He advised me to go that very hour to the Lieutenant of Police and to the Provost of Paris. I went, but to my final misfortune; for not only did this step and the efforts made by the two Officers of Justice avail me nothing, but I gave Lescaut opportunity to talk with his sister, and inspire her during my absence with a horrible resolve. He spoke to her of M. de G . . . M . . ., an old voluptuary who paid lavishly for his pleasures, and pictured to her so many advantages in placing herself on his pay list, that, troubled as she was by our disaster, she entered into all the arguments with which he plied her. This honourable bargain was concluded before my return, and the fulfilment postponed till the morrow, when Lescaut should have sounded M. de G . . . M . . . . I found him waiting for me at my house; but Manon had gone to bed in her own room, and had given orders to her lackey to tell me that being in need of a little rest, she begged me to leave her alone for that night. Lescaut left me, after offering me a few pistoles, which I accepted. It was almost four o'clock when I went to bed, and even then, occupied as I was in revolving schemes to restore my fortunes, I fell asleep so late that I did not waken until towards eleven next morning. I got up hurriedly and went to see how Manon was: I was told that she had gone out an hour before with her brother, who had come to fetch her in a hackney coach. Although such an expedition with Lescaut seemed to me mysterious, I did myself violence to keep my suspicion in abeyance. I suffered several hours to pass, which I spent in reading. Then, no longer able to master my uneasiness, I began to pace up and down our rooms. In that of Manon I noticed a sealed letter lying on her table. It was addressed to me, and the writing was in her hand. I opened it, with a mortal shudder. It was as follows:

I swear to you, dear Chevalier, that you are the idol of my heart and that there is no one in the world I could love in the way I love you; but do you not see, my poor dear heart, that in the state to which we are reduced, fidelity is a silly virtue? Do you think one can make love when one has nothing to eat? Hunger would cheat me to death; some day I should give my last sigh and think it was for love. I adore you, be sure of that: but leave me for a little while to contrive our fortunes. Unlucky the man who is to fall into my snare! I am working to make my Chevalier rich and happy. My brother will bring you news of your Manon, and tell you how she cried at being forced to leave you.

I remained after reading it in a state that I can hardly describe, for I know not even now what were the first emotions by which I was shaken. It was one of these unique situations, to which one has experienced no parallel; one could not explain them to others, because they have no conception of it, and it is all one can do to unravel them for one's self, because, being alone of their kind, there is no connecting link of memory, and no relation with any familiar sentiment. However, whatever my emotions may have been, certain it is that among them must have entered grief, resentment, jealousy and shame. Too happy, if among them had not also been love! She loves me, I can well believe it; but would she not be a monster, I cried, if she were to hate me? What rights were ever held upon a heart that I might not claim upon hers? What was there left to do for her, after all that I have given up for her? Yet she deserts me, and graceless, she thinks herself safe from my reproaches by telling me that she has not ceased to love me. She is afraid of hunger: God of Love! what grossness of feeling, and how ill a response to my delicacy! I feared it not at all, I who exposed myself thereto so willingly for her, when I gave up my fortune and all the sweetness of my father's house: I who denied myself even necessities to satisfy her passing humour and caprice. She adores me, says she. Ah, most unkind, had you indeed adored me, I know whose counsel you would have sought; at least you would not have left me without saying farewell. It is I who can tell what cruel pains there are in being separated from what one adores. One must have lost one's wits before voluntarily exposing one's self thereto.

My complaints were interrupted by a visit which I had not expected: that of Lescaut. Hangman! said I, my hand on my sword, where is Manon? what have you done with her? My gesture alarmed him: he made answer that if this were his reception when he came to give me an account of the most important service he could render me, he would take his departure and never set foot in my house again. Do not imagine, said I, turning upon him, that you can make me again your dupe and trick me by fairy-tales; look to your life, or find me Manon. Lord, but you are hot upon it, said he; that is precisely what brings me. I came to tell you a piece of luck you never thought of, and for which you will perhaps acknowledge that you owe me some gratitude. I would have him enlighten me there and then. He told me that Manon, unable to endure the fear of poverty, and above all the thought of having all at once to retrench, had begged him to introduce her to M. de G . . . M . . ., who had the reputation of being free-handed. He took care not to tell me that the advice had come from him, and that he had prepared the way before bringing her thereto. I took her there this morning, said he, and the good man was so charmed by her quality that he has invited her first to keep him company at his country house, where he has gone to spend a few days. I, added Lescaut, realising at once what advantage might be in this for you, hinted to him that Manon had suffered heavy losses, and so far stirred his generosity that he began by making her a present of two hundred pistoles. I said to him that that was handsome enough for the present, but that the future would bring my sister heavy obligations: that she was moreover burdened with the care of a young brother who had been left on our hands after the death of our father and mother, and that, if he judged her worthy of his regard, he would not permit her to suffer in the person of this poor child, whom she looked on as half herself. This tale did not fail to move him; he has promised to rent a suitable house for you and for Manon: for it is you who are the poor little brother, so much to be pitied; he has promised to fit you out and supply you every month with a good four hundred *livres*, which will mean, if I am right in my count, four thousand eight hundred at the end of the year. He has left orders with his steward, before setting out for his country house, to look for a house and have it ready against his return. Then you will see Manon again: she charged me to embrace you for her a thousand times, and assure you that she loves you more than ever.

I sat down, mazed at this fantastic ordering of my lot: I found myself torn between opposed feelings and consequently in an uncertainty so difficult to put an end to, that I remained for long enough deaf to the questions which Lescaut put to me one upon the other. It was at this moment that honour and virtue made me suffer once again the pangs of remorse, and that I turned my eyes wistfully towards Amiens, towards my father's house, towards Saint-Sulpice, towards every spot where I had lived in innocence. By how vast a gulf was I not separated from that happy state? I saw it now but from a great way off, like a shadow which still drew my regrets and desires, but too faint to rouse me to effort. By what fatality, said I, have I become so criminal? Love is an innocent passion; how has it been changed for me into a source of misery and disorder? Who hindered me from living peacefully and virtuously with Manon? Why did I not marry her before obtaining aught of her love? My father loved me so tenderly—would he not have consented to it if I had urged him with legitimate insistence! Ah! my father would himself have cherished her as a charming girl, only too good for his son. I should be happy with the love of Manon, my father's affection, the regard of honourable men, the gifts of fortune and the tranquillity which goodness gives. Oh sinister contrast! What infamous rôle is this which has just been proposed to me? What! that I should go to share. . . . But can one hesitate if it was Manon who ordered it thus, and if without this complaisance I shall lose her? M. Lescaut, I cried, closing my eyes as if to escape from thoughts so torturing, if you were minded to do me a service, I thank you for it: you might have found a more honourable way, but the thing is over and done, is it not? Now then, let's think no more but of profiting by your pains and carrying out your plan. Lescaut, who had been considerably perturbed by my wrath, and then by my silence, was enchanted to find me in a mood so different from that which he had for the last few moments feared: he was anything but courageous, as I was to prove still more conclusively in the sequel. Yes, yes, he hastened to reply, it is a right good service I have done you, and you will see that we will get more profit out of it than you think. We began to devise by what means we could dissipate any suspicions which M. de G . . . M . . . might entertain of my being her brother, on seeing me taller and a little older perhaps than he imagined me. We found no better plan than for me to behave with him like an innocent lad from the provinces, and to make him believe that it was my intention to take Orders, and was therefore going every day to college. We decided moreover that I would acquit myself very awkwardly on the first occasion that I should be given the honour of meeting him. He came back to town three or four days later, and himself brought Manon to the house which his steward had had instructions to make ready. She sent to inform Lescaut of her return, and the latter having sent me word, we both appeared that evening at her house. Her elderly lover had already gone out.

Despite the resignation with which I had submitted to her will, I could not repress the plaint in my heart at seeing her again. She found me sad and spiritless. The joy of finding her once more could not wholly prevail over distress at her faithlessness. She, on the contrary, seemed transported with delight at seeing me again; she reproached me for my coldness. I could not refrain from letting fall the words false and faithless, and with them as many sighs. She bantered me at first on my childishness; but when she saw my gaze still sorrowfully fixed upon her, and the pain it cost me to endure a change so contrary to my humour and my desires, she passed alone into her chamber. I followed her in a moment. I found her all in tears. I asked her the cause of them. You might see it easily enough, said she, how am I to live if the sight of me can only make you look dismal and vexed? You have been here an hour, and have not given me a single kiss, and you have suffered mine with the majesty of the Grand Turk in his Seraglio. Listen, Manon, said I, taking her in my arms, I cannot hide from you that my heart is in deadly grief. I say nothing now of the alarm into which your sudden flight threw me, nor of your cruelty in abandoning me without a word of comfort, after spending the night apart from me. The charm of your presence would make me forget more than that. But do you imagine that I could think without sighs, and even without tears, I went on, while some fell from my eyes, on the sad and wretched life you would have me lead in this house? Put on one side my birth and my honour; they are considerations too weak to rival a love such as mine: but that very love, can you not conceive how it must groan to see itself so ill rewarded, I dare not say so tyrannously abused by a thankless and hard-hearted mistress? . . . She interrupted me. Stop, Chevalier, said she: it is no use to torment me by reproaches that pierce my heart when it is you who utter them. I see what wounds you. I had hoped that you might consent to the plan I had made to restore our fortune, and it was to spare your delicacy that I began to carry it into execution without your knowledge; but I give it up, since you do not approve of it. She added that she would only ask a little complaisance from me for the rest of the day; that

~ 50 ~

she had already received two hundred pistoles from her elderly lover: that he had promised to bring her that evening a beautiful pearl necklace, with other pieces of jewellery, and in addition half of the yearly allowance he had promised her. Do but give me time, said she, to receive his gifts; I swear to you that he will not have the satisfaction of having spent a single night with me, for I had put him off until now when we should be in town. It is true that he has kissed my hands a million times over; it is only fair that he should pay for that pleasure, and it would not be dear at five or six thousand francs, if you proportion the price to his riches and his age.

Her resolution was far more agreeable to me than the hope of the five thousand pounds. I had time to recognise that my heart was not yet lost to every sentiment of honour, since it was so content to have escaped infamy. But I was born to brief joys and lasting sorrows. Fortune delivered me from one abyss only to hurl me into another. When I had signified to Manon by a thousand caresses how happy I counted myself at her change of plan, I said to her that we must tell M. Lescaut, so that our measures might be taken in concert. He grumbled at first; but the four or five thousand pounds of ready money made him fall in with our plan. It was then agreed that we should all three be there to sup with M. de G ... M ..., and that for two reasons; one, to give us the pleasure of an amusing scene, in my passing myself off as a schoolboy brother of Manon's; the other, to keep the old rake from taking over much freedom with my mistress, by the right which he might think he had acquired by so liberal payment in advance. M. Lescaut and I should have to retire, when he went up to the room where he counted on spending the night, and Manon, instead of following him, promised to come out and to spend it with me. Lescaut took it upon him to have a coach just at the door.

The supper hour at hand, M. de G ... M ... did not long keep us waiting. Lescaut was with his sister in the salon. The first com-

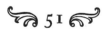

pliment of the old man was to offer his fair one a necklace, bracelet and pendants of pearls, worth at least a hundred pistoles. He then counted out to her in good *louis d'or*, the sum of two thousand four hundred *livres*, which represented the half of her allowance. He seasoned his present with a certain number of caresses in the taste of the old Court. Manon could not refuse him a few kisses; they were so many rights acquired by the money which he laid in her hands. I was at the door where I stood listening, waiting till Lescaut should bid me come in. He came and took me by the hand, when Manon had locked away the money and the jewels: leading me towards M. de G . . . M . . ., he bade me make my bow. I made him two or three of the deepest. Excuse him, sir, said Lescaut, it is a callow youngster. He is very far, as you see, from Paris breeding; but we hope that a little experience will form him. You will have the honour of seeing Monsieur here often, he added, turning to me, see to it that you profit by so fine a model. The elderly lover seemed to be pleased to see me. He tapped me twice or thrice on the cheek, saying that I was a pretty lad, but that I must be on my guard in Paris, where young folk very easily fall into bad ways. Lescaut assured him that I was naturally so good that I talked of nothing but becoming a priest, and that my whole delight was in building little Chapels. I find a look of Manon in him, said the old man, tilting up my chin with his hand. Sir, said I, innocently, it is because we are so near in flesh, and I love my sister Manon as if she were my other self. You hear that? said he to Lescaut. He has wit. It is a pity that the youngster has not seen a little more of the world. Oh Monsieur, said I, I have seen plenty of it in the Churches at home, and I am pretty sure that I shall find bigger fools in Paris than I am. There now, said he, that is passing well for a boy from the Provinces. Our whole conversation at supper was much the same. Manon who was in a roguish mood was several times on the verge of spoiling all by her bursts of laughter. I found opportunity while at supper to tell him his own story and the ill fate that hung over him. Lescaut and Manon quailed as the tale went on, above all when I sketched his own portrait to the life: but his vanity kept him from recognising himself, and I sketched it so adroitly that he was the first to find it highly comical. You will see that it is not without reason I have dwelt on this ridiculous scene. At length, the hour of retiring come, he proposed to Manon to go to bed. Lescaut and I took our departure. He was conducted to his room, and Manon, slipping out on some pretext, came and joined us at the door. The coach which was waiting three or four houses down, drove up for us. In a moment we had left the quarter behind us.

To my mind, this proceeding was knavish enough. Yet it was not the most unjustifiable that I had to reproach myself with. I had more scruples as to the money I had won at cards. However, we profited as little by the one as by the other, and Heaven suffered that the lighter of the two wrongs should be the more rigorously punished. M. de G . . . M . . . was not slow to realise that he had been duped. I do not know whether he did not, that very night, take steps to find us: but he had influence enough not to be baulked for long, and we imprudence enough to count too much on the size of Paris and the distance between our quarter and his. Not only was he informed of our whereabouts and of our immediate affairs, but he also learned who I was, the life I had led in Paris, Manon's former connection with B . . ., the trick she had played upon him; in a word, all the scandalous particulars of our story. He thereupon came to the decision to have us arrested, and treated less as criminals than arrant adventurers. We were still in bed when an officer from the Lieutenant of Police entered our room with half a dozen Guards. They first of all seized our money, or rather that of M. de G . . . M . . ., and, ordering us roughly to get up, conducted us to the door where we found two coaches, in one of which poor Manon was driven off to the Common Hospital, and myself in the other to

Saint-Lazare. It requires actual experience of such reverses to judge of the despair which they can produce. Our Guards had the harshness to refuse to allow me to embrace Manon, or even say a word to her. For a long time I did not know what had become of her. Doubtless it was fortunate that I did not know at first, for so terrible a catastrophe might have made me lose my senses, perhaps my life.

My unfortunate mistress, then, was carried off to the Hôpital. What a fate for a creature so charming, who would have graced the first throne in the world if all men had seen her with my eyes and my heart! She was not treated with barbarity, but she was shut up in close confinement alone, and condemned to accomplish each day a certain quantity of work, as the condition of obtaining some revolting nourishment. I only learned these facts long afterwards, when I had myself endured several months of hard and weary penance. My guards being equally reticent as to the place where they had orders to conduct me, I did not know my fate, till I was at the gate of Saint-Lazare. I should have preferred death, at that moment, to the condition in which I thought myself about to fall. I had the most terrifying idea of that house. My fears increased when on entering my guards a second time went through my pockets, to make sure that I was left with no weapons or means of defence. The Superior at once appeared: he had been apprised of my coming. He greeted me with a good deal of kindness. Father, said I, let me have no indignities. I shall die a thousand deaths before I submit to any. No, no, Monsieur, he replied, let your conduct be good, and we shall be very well pleased with one another. He requested me to go up to an upper room. I followed him without resistance. The Archers accompanied us as far as the door, and the Superior, entering with me, motioned to them to withdraw.

So then, I am your prisoner? said I. Well, Father, what do you mean to do with me? He told me that he was delighted to find me take a sensible tone: that his duty would be to labour to inspire me with some relish for virtue and religion, and mine to profit by his exhortations and his counsels: that if I would but respond however little to the consideration he would show me, I should find only pleasure in my solitude. Ah! Pleasure! I retorted, you do not know, Father, the one thing that can give me that! I do know it, he replied, but I hope that your inclinations will alter. His reply made me think that he must know my story, and perhaps my name. I begged him to tell me if it were so. He answered simply that he had been informed of everything. This knowledge was my severest chastisement. I began to shed a torrent of tears, with all the tokens of a terrible despair. I could not be comforted for a humiliation that must make me the byword of my whole acquaintance and the disgrace of my family. I passed thus a whole week in the most utter prostration, incapable of understanding or of occupying myself with anything but my own disgrace. Even the memory of Manon added nothing to my grief. At most, it entered into it only as a sentiment which had preceded this new anguish, and the dominant passion of my soul was shame and confusion. There are few who know the power of these particular emotions of the heart. The generality of men are sensible only of five or six passions, within whose circle their lives are spent, and round which all their perturbations centre. Take from them love and hate, pleasure and pain, hope and fear, and they feel no longer. But those of a certain temper are liable to be stirred in a thousand different ways: they seem to have more than the five senses, and to be capable of receiving ideas and impressions which lie beyond the ordinary confines of nature. And as they have a consciousness of greatness which raises them above the crowd, so is there nothing of which they are more jealous. Thence comes it that they take so ill with contempt and ridicule, and that shame is one of the most violent of their passions.

I had this sorry advantage at Saint-Lazare. My dejection seemed so excessive to the Superior that fearing its possible consequences he felt he must treat me with a good deal of gentleness and indulgence. He came to see me twice or thrice in the day. He brought me often with him to take a turn in the garden, and his zeal exhausted itself in exhortations and in wholesome advice. I received them with gentleness, I even showed signs of gratitude, from which he began to draw hope of my conversion. You are so gentle, so lovable by nature, said he one day, that I cannot understand the disorders of which they accuse you. Two things amaze me, one, that with so many good qualities you could so abandon yourself to the extremes of debauch; and the other, at which I marvel still more, you can receive so willingly my counsels and instructions after having lived for years in habits of disorder. If it is repentance, you are a notable example of the tender mercy of Heaven: if it is natural goodness, you have at any rate an excellent foundation of moral rectitude, which makes me hope that we shall not need to keep you long here to restore you to an honourable and ordered life. I was enchanted to find him in this way of thinking. I resolved to encourage it by a behaviour which might satisfy him wholly, convinced that this was the surest way of shortening my imprisonment. I asked him for books. He was surprised that, the choice of what I should read being left to me, I decided on several serious and Christian Authors. I pretended to apply myself to study with the utmost devotion, and provided him, at every opportunity, with proofs of the change which he desired.

Nevertheless, it was outward only. I confess it to my shame, but the rôle which I played at Saint-Lazare was that of hypocrite. Instead of studying when I was alone, I occupied myself only with bewailing my fate. I would curse my prison and the tyranny which held me there. No sooner had I in the least revived from the prostration into which my disgrace had thrown me, than I fell again into the torments of love. The absence of Manon, the uncertainty as to her fate, the fear of never seeing her more, were the only objects of my sorrowful cogitations. I pictured her in the arms of M. de G... M... for that had been my first thought: and far from imagining that he had dealt out to her the same treatment as to myself, I was convinced that he had only had me removed so as to possess her undisturbed. In this fashion I spent days and nights which seemed to me eternal. My only hope was in the success of my hypocrisy. I took careful note of the face and conversation of the Superior to ascertain what he thought of me, and I made it my study to please him as the arbiter of my destiny. It was easy to see that I stood very high in his favour. I no longer doubted but that he would be disposed to do me service. I had the boldness to ask him one day if it were upon him that my enlargement depended. He told me that he was not absolute master of it: but that, on his recommendation, he hoped that M. de G... M..., at whose solicitation the Lieutenant-General of Police had had me imprisoned, would agree to set me at liberty. Might I flatter myself, I continued humbly, that the two months of prison which I have already endured will seem to him sufficient expiation? He promised to speak of it to him if I wished, and I begged him earnestly to do me this kindness. Two days later he told me that G... M... had been so touched by the good report he had of me that not only did he seem inclined to let me again see daylight, but that he had even shown a strong wish to know me better, and proposed to pay me a visit in my prison. Although his presence could not be agreeable to me, I looked upon it as a step to liberty.

He did indeed come to Saint-Lazare. His manner seemed to me graver and less foppish than it had been in Manon's apartment. He made me several very sensible speeches on my bad behaviour, and added, presumably to justify his own disorders, that it is permitted the weakness of mankind to provide themselves with certain pleasures which nature demands, but that knavery and disgraceful practices deserve their punishment. I listened to him with a submissiveness that seemed to please him. I did not even take offence at certain quips which were levelled at my brotherly relation with Lescaut and Manon, and on the little Chapels which he supposed, said he, I must have made plenty of at Saint-Lazare, since I took so much pleasure in this pious occupation. But it slipped from him, unfortunately for him and for me, that Manon must doubtless have made very pretty ones too at the Hôpital. In spite of the shuddering which that name sent through me, I had enough self-control to beg him humbly to explain himself. Indeed yes, said he, for two months now she has been learning to behave herself at the Common Hospital, and I wish she may have profited by it as much as you have at Saint-Lazare.

Even had perpetual imprisonment or death itself been held before my eyes, I could not have mastered my frenzy at that frightful news. I hurled myself upon him in rage so furious that it took half my strength from me. Enough was left me, however, to throw him on the ground and seize him by the throat. I was throttling him, when the noise of his fall and the few sharp cries which I had scarcely left him liberty to utter attracted the Superior and several Monks to my room. They took him from me. I was myself all but exhausted. I could hardly breathe. My God! I moaned. Just Heaven! am I to live after such infamy? I made another attempt to fling myself upon the brute who had just dealt me my death blow. They held me back. My despair, my cries and tears passed all imagining. So frantic were my gestures, that the bystanders, who knew nothing of the cause, exchanged glances as much in alarm as in astonishment. Meantime M. de G . . . M . . . was readjusting his wig and his cravate, and in his spite at the mauling he had suffered, gave orders to the Superior to confine me more closely than ever, and to chastise me by all the means which are known to be in use at Saint-Lazare. Not so, Monsieur, replied the Superior, it is not for a person of the Chevalier's rank to be used in such fashion. He is so

"I could not master my frenzy at that frightful news. I hurled myself upon him in rage so furious that it took half my strength from me"

gentle, moreover, and so courteous that I can hardly conceive of his flying to such extremes without good reason for it. This reply succeeded in putting M. de G . . . M . . . thoroughly out of countenance. He took his departure, declaring that he would find means to humble both the Superior and myself, and any man who had the audacity to oppose him.

The Superior, bidding the Brethren see him to the door, remained alone with me. He conjured me to acquaint him at once with what had led to such an outbreak. O Father! I cried, still crying like a child, think of the cruellest deed, the most detestable piece of savagery you can conceive of: that is what this infamous G . . . M . . . has just been scoundrel enough to do. He has stabbed me to the heart, I shall never get over it: I want to tell you everything. I went on, sobbing, you are kind, you will have pity on me. I gave him a brief account of the long and insurmountable passion which I felt for Manon: of the flourishing state of our fortunes just before our own servants stripped us bare: of the proposals which G . . . M . . . had made to my mistress: of the settlement of their bargain and the fashion which it had been broken off. I set the facts before him, I confess, in the light most favourable to ourselves. There, said I, is the source of M. de G . . . M . . .'s zeal for my reformation. He had influence enough to have me shut up here out of motives of sheer revenge; I can forgive him for it, but, Father, alas! that is not all. He had the dearest half of myself carried off: he has had her shamefully committed to the Hôpital, he had the impudence to tell me so to-day with his own lips. To the Hôpital, Father! Heavens! my lovely mistress, my dearest Queen at the Hôpital, like the foulest of all creatures! Where shall I find strength to endure a thing so monstrous and not die? The good Father, seeing me in such extremity of misery, did his best to comfort me. He told me that he had never had the rights of my story as I told it: that he had known, indeed, that my life was irregular, but had imagined that the reason of M. de G . . . M . . .'s interest in me was some bond of esteem and affection with my family; that he had only been able to explain the situation to himself on this footing; that what I had just told him must effect a very considerable change in my affairs, and that he had no doubt but the faithful account of them which he meant to give the Lieutenant-General of Police must surely assist towards my liberation. He then asked me why I had never as yet thought of giving any news of myself to my family, since they had had nothing whatever to do with my imprisonment. I satisfied him on this point, arguing the pain which I had feared to cause my father, and the shame which I should have suffered therein myself. Finally he promised me to go without dallying to the Lieutenant of Police, if it were only, he added, to forestall something worse on the part of M. de G . . . M . . ., who quitted this house in a very ill humour, and who has consideration enough to be formidable.

I awaited the good Father's return with all the agitation of a poor wretch who momentarily expects to hear sentence pronounced upon him. To imagine Manon at the Hôpital was torture indescribable. Apart from the infamy attached to the place, I had no knowledge as to how she was being treated there, and the memory of some details which I had heard of that house of fear came back every moment to revive my agony. So determined was I to rescue her, whatever the means, that if every other way of leaving it had failed me, I should have set fire to Saint-Lazare. I set myself then to consider what steps I must take, if it should happen that the Lieutenant-General continued to hold me against my will. I applied my ingenuity to all contrivances: I exhausted every possibility. Not one of them seemed to promise me a certain escape, and I feared stricter confinement if I came to grief in a first attempt. I called to mind the names of various friends whose help I might hope for: but how was I ever to send them news of me? In the end, I believed that I had contrived a plan so ingenious that it must succeed, and I postponed the still more complete arranging of it till the return of the Father Superior, should the failure of his errand render it necessary. He was not slow in returning. I could not see on his countenance those signs of pleasure which accompany good tidings. I have spoken, said he, with the Lieutenant-General of Police, but I spoke too late. M. de G . . . M . . . had gone to see him after leaving here, and had so strongly prejudiced him against you that he was on the point of sending me fresh orders to confine you more closely.

However, when I let him know the real truth of your affairs, he seemed to grow more human: and with a passing jest at the incontinence of old M. de G . . . M . . . he said that you must be left here for six months to satisfy him, and so much the better, he added, since your sojourn here cannot fail to be of advantage to you. He recommended me to treat you with consideration, and I assure you that you shall have nothing to complain of my methods.

The good Superior's explanation was long enough to give me time for one wise reflection. I realised that I should run the risk of upsetting my plans if I showed myself too eager for my liberty. I assured him, on the contrary, that in the necessity of my longer sojourn, I had the happy consolation of having some share in his regard. I then begged him, in all sincerity, to do me a favour which was of no moment to anyone else and would much avail to my tranquillity: it was to send word to one of my friends, a saintly ecclesiastic living at Saint-Sulpice, that I was at Saint-Lazare, and to allow me sometimes to receive an edifying visit from him. This favour was granted me without hesitation. It was my friend Tiberge of whom I spoke: not that I could hope to win from him any assistance towards my liberation, but it was my thought to use him as an indirect instrument thereto, without his being aware of it. In a word, this was my plan: I wished to write to Lescaut, and to charge him, along with our mutual friends, with the task of setting me free. The first difficulty was in getting the letter to his hands:

this was to be the office of Tiberge. However, as he knew him to be brother to my mistress, I feared that he would have scruples in undertaking the commission. My design was to enclose my letter to Lescaut in another letter which I should address to a worthy man of my acquaintance, begging him to convey the former without delay to its address: and as it was essential that I should see Lescaut in order that our plans might coincide, I would instruct him to come to Saint-Lazare, and ask to see me under the name of my elder brother who should have come to Paris expressly to find out how I did. I left it to our meeting to decide whatever plans might seem to us speediest and surest. On the morrow, the Father Superior sent word to Tiberge of my desire to talk with him. This faithful friend had not so far lost me from his sight that he was unaware of what had befallen me: he knew that I was at Saint-Lazare, and perhaps had not been over distressed at a disgrace which might, he thought, bring me back again to duty. He hurried at once to my chamber.

Our conversation was full of affection. He was eager to know the state of my mind. I opened my heart to him without reserve, except as regarded my plans for flight. It is not in your eyes, dear friend, said I, that I would appear to be what I am not. If you had thought to find a friend become wise and discreet in his desires, a libertine aroused by the chastisements of heaven, a heart, in a word, set free from love and recovered from the charm of his Manon, you judged me too favourably. You see me again just as you left me four months ago: still fond, and still unhappy in that fatal passion wherein is all my hope of happiness. He made answer that the confession I had just made left me without excuse: that there were plenty of Sinners so intoxicated with the false pleasure of Vice as to prefer it far over that of virtue, but it was at least to a show of happiness that they clung, they were the dupes of appearances; but to recognise as I did that the object of my desires was capable only of making me guilty and unhappy, and to continue in deliberately plunging myself into misfortune and crime, was a contradiction of ideas and conduct which did small honour to my powers of reason. Tiberge, I returned, it is an easy victory, when there is no one to resist your arms! Let me reason a little in my turn. Can you claim that what you call the happiness of virtue is exempt from pain, from obstacles and from annoyances? What name will you give to imprisonment, to the cross, to the executions and tortures of tyrants? Will you say, as do the Mystics, that that which torments the body is happiness to the soul? You would not dare to say it; it is an untenable paradox. This happiness which you so extol is alloyed with a thousand pains; or to speak more accurately, it is but a web of misfortunes through which one aims at felicity. Now, if the power of imagination can find pleasure in these very evils, because they may lead to the happy issue of one's hopes, why do you treat the precisely similar disposition, in my behaviour, as contradictory and insensate? I love Manon: I aim, through a thousand griefs, at living in peace and happiness by her side. The way by which I go is dolorous, but the hope of arriving at my destination sheds sweetness on it, and I should think myself overpaid, by one moment spent with her, for all the miseries that I endure to win it. Things seem to me evenly balanced, on your side and on mine: or if there is any difference, it is to my advantage: for the happiness that I speak of is close at hand, the other a great way off: mine is of the same quality as the pains, that is to say, the body is sensible of it: and the other is of a quality unknown, and assured only to faith.

Tiberge seemed appalled by this reasoning. He recoiled a pace or two, saying with extreme gravity that what I had just said not only outraged common sense, but was an unhappy piece of sophistry, impious and irreligious: for this comparison, he added, of the issue of your afflictions with that which is indicated by religion, is an idea of the most libertine and most monstrous kind. I confess, said I, that it is not exact: but remember, it is not upon that that my argument depends. It was my design to explain what seems to you a contradiction in the persistence of an unhappy passion: and I think I have sufficiently proved that if there is one, you could save yourself from it no more than I. It is only in this respect that I have treated these matters as equivalent, and I still maintain that they are so. Do you reply that the end of virtue is infinitely superior to that of love? Who will not agree to that? But is that the matter in dispute? Is it not rather the ability which both alike possess to endure pain? Judge by results: how many deserters will you find from a rigid virtue, and how few from love? Again, do you reply that if there are difficulties in the exercise of good, they are not inevitable and necessary? that there are no longer Tyrants and crosses to be found, and that plenty of good people may be seen living a life of ease and tranquillity? Even so, I shall answer, are there loves which are peaceful and fortunate: and, yet another difference very much in my favour, I shall add that love, although it too often deceives, at all events promises naught but joys and satisfaction, whereas religion will have you count only upon a course of dolour and mortification. Do not be alarmed, I added, seeing his ardour about to turn to vexation, the only conclusion I would draw here is that there is no worse method to disgust a heart with love, than to decry its sweetness, and promise it more happiness in the exercise of virtue. Made as we are, it is certain that felicity for us consists in pleasure; I challenge any other definition of it; now the heart has no need long to question itself, to feel that of all pleasures the sweetest are those of love. It soon knows itself cheated, if it is promised others more charming elsewhere, and that deception disposes it to mistrust the most solid assurance. You preachers who would fain bring me back to virtue, tell me that it is indispensably necessary: but do not disguise the fact that it is harsh and painful. Prove as you may that the delights of love are transient, that they are forbidden, that they will be followed by eternal pain, and, what will perhaps make more impression on me, that the sweeter, the dearer they are, the more magnificent the reward of Heaven for so great a sacrifice: but confess that, given hearts such as ours, they are the most perfect felicity that this world may know. This conclusion to my discourse restored Tiberge to good humour. He agreed that there was some reason in my way of thinking. The only objection which he made was to ask me why I did not follow at least my own precepts, by sacrificing my love to the hope of that recompense of which I had formed so exalted an idea. Ah dear friend! I answered, it is here that I own my misery and my weakness. Alas! it is indeed my duty to act according to my reasoning: but is action in my power? What aid should I not require if I am to forget the charms of Manon? God forgive me! said Tiberge, here I think is another of our Jansenists! I do not know what I am, I made answer, and I do not know too well what a Jansenist may be, but I find only too shrewdly the truth of what they say.

This conversation served at least to revive my friend's compassion. He realised that there was more weakness than malignity in my disorders and his friendship was the more disposed to give me in the end the aid without which I should infallibly have died of misery. Nevertheless I gave him not the smallest inkling of the plan which I had formed of escaping from Saint-Lazare. I begged him only to take charge of my letter. I had it ready before he came, and I did not lack excuses to colour the necessity which I was in to write it. He had the good faith to deliver it precisely, and before the end of the day Lescaut had received the letter intended for himself. He came to see me the next day, and was able luckily to pass as my brother. My joy was extreme when I saw him enter my chamber. I shut the door carefully. Let us not lose a moment, said I; first give me news of Manon, and then give me counsel how to break my fetters. He assured me that he had not seen his sister since the day that had preceded my imprisonment: that he had only learned her fate and mine by dint of earnest investigation: that he had gone twice or thrice to the Hôpital, and had been refused permission to speak to her. Accursed G . . . M . . ., I cried, you will pay dear for this!

As far as your own liberation is concerned, went on Lescaut, it is not so easy an undertaking as you think. We went past this place yesterday evening, two of my friends and I, to take note of all the outer parts of the house, and we decided that since your windows give on a courtyard surrounded by buildings, as you had told us, there would be a good deal of difficulty in getting you out of it. Besides, you are on the third floor, and we could not smuggle in either cords or ladders. I can see no help from outside; it is in the house itself that we must imagine some trick. No, I replied, I have examined everything, especially since my confinement grew less strict, thanks to the Superior's indulgence. The door of my room is now left unlocked; I have liberty to walk up and down the Monks' corridors: but all the staircases are blocked by heavy doors which are carefully kept closed day and night, so that it is impossible for adroitness alone to save me. Wait! I went on, after reflecting a moment on an idea which seemed to me excellent, could you bring me a pistol? Easily, said Lescaut, but do you want to kill someone? I assured him that I had so little intention of killing anyone that the pistol need not even be loaded. Bring it to me to-morrow, said I, and do not fail to be here, at eleven o'clock that night, opposite the door of this house, with two or three of our friends. I hope to be able to join you. He urged me in vain to tell him more. I told him that such an enterprise as I had in mind could only seem reasonable after it had come off. I begged him to cut short his visit, that he might find it easier to see me again next day. He was admitted with as little difficulty as at first; his air was dignified: no one but would have taken him for an honourable gentleman.

Once the instrument of my freedom was in my hands, I had

little doubt as to the success of my plan. It was fantastic and daring: but given the motives that inspired me, was there anything of which I was not capable? I had observed, since I had been allowed to go out of my room and walk up and down the corridors, that the Porter every evening brought the keys of all the doors to the Superior, after which a profound silence reigned throughout the house, a token that everyone had gone to bed. I could go without any hindrance, by a communicating passage, from my room to that of the Father. My determination was to take the keys from him, terrifying him with my Pistol, if he made any difficulty in giving me them, and use them to gain the street. I awaited the moment with impatience. The Porter came at the usual hour, a little after nine o'clock. I let still another hour go by, to make sure that all the Brethren and the servants were asleep. At last I set out, with my weapon and a lighted candle. I knocked gently at first on the Father's door so as to awaken him without noise. He heard me at the second knock, and imagining doubtless that it was one of the Brethren who was taken ill and had need of aid, he got out of bed to open to me. He took the precaution however of asking through the door who it was and what was wanted of him. I was compelled to say who I was, but I assumed a plaintive voice, to convey to him that I did not feel well. Ah, it is you, my dear son, said he, opening the door. Now, what is it brings you so late? I entered the room, and having brought him to the other end, opposite the door, I declared that I could not endure to stay longer at Saint-Lazare; that the night was a convenient time to go out without being observed, and that I counted on his friendship to consent to open the doors for me, or lend me his keys to open them myself.

This compliment was bound to surprise him. He remained for some time gazing at me without reply; but as I had no time to lose, I began again by saying that I was indeed touched by all his kindnesses, but that liberty being the dearest of all good things, above all to me from whom it had been unjustly reft, I was determined to procure it for myself that same night, whatever it might cost, and for fear that it might occur to him to raise his voice to call for help, I showed him the good reason for silence that I held under my tunic. A pistol! said he. What! my son, do you mean to take my life in return for the consideration I have shown you? God forbid! said I. You have too much intelligence and good sense to drive me to that: but I mean to be free, and I am so set upon it that if my plan fails through your fault, it is all up with you. But, my dear son, he replied, his face white and terrified, what have I done? What reason have you to desire my death? I tell you, none, I retorted, impatiently. I have no intention of killing you if you wish to live; open the door for me, and I am your best friend. I observed the keys lying on his table. I took them and begged him to follow me, making as little noise as possible. He was forced to bring himself to it. Regularly as we advanced and as he would open a door, he repeated to me with a sigh, Oh, my son! who would ever have believed it? Not a sound, Father, I repeated every moment in return. At length we arrived at a kind of barrier which stood before the great door into the street. I thought myself already free, and I was behind the Father with my candle in one hand and my pistol in the other. Whilst he was busied opening it, a Servant who slept in a little room close by, hearing the noise of several bolts, got up and put his head out of the door. The good Father evidently judged him capable of stopping me. He ordered him very imprudently to come to his help. He was a powerful fellow, and rushed upon me without hesitation. I did not stop to bargain, I shot him through the chest. See what you have done, Father, said I to the Superior: but do not let it hinder you from finishing, I added, pushing him towards the last door. He dared not refuse to open it. I came happily out, and a few paces away found Lescaut who was awaiting me with two friends, according to his pledge.

We made off. Lescaut asked me if he had not heard a pistol-shot. That is your fault, said I, why did you bring it to me loaded? Nevertheless I thanked him for having taken that precaution, failing which I should doubtless have been long enough at Saint-Lazare. We went to spend the night at a Tavern where I made up a little for the poor cheer I had had for the last three months. Yet I could not give myself up to pleasure. I was suffering mortally in Manon. She must be set free, said I to my three friends. It was only for that that I wished my own liberty. I ask the aid of your skill. For my own part, I shall stake life itself. Lescaut, who was not lacking in intelligence or prudence, put it to me that we must feel our way; that my escape from Saint-Lazare and the piece of ill-luck that had befallen me as I came out, would infallibly cause some stir: that the Lieutenant-General of Police would call a search, and that he had a long arm; in short that if I did not wish to find myself enduring something worse than Saint-Lazare, it would be wise to keep close and hidden for several days, to give the first flame of my enemies' wrath time to die out. His advice was wise; but it would have required equal wisdom to follow it. Such tardiness and circumspection accorded ill with my passion. The utmost of my compliance was to promise him that I would spend the following day in sleeping. He shut me into my room, where I remained until evening.

I spent part of this time in devising plans and expedients to rescue Manon. I was convinced that her prison was even more inaccessible than mine had been. There could be no question of force or violence. A trick must serve us; but the very goddess of invention would not have known where to begin. I could see so little light that I put off my better consideration of things till I should have learned some particulars of the internal arrangements of the Hôpital. As soon as night had brought darkness, I begged Lescaut to accompany me. We got into conversation with one of the

Porters, who seemed a sensible man. I pretended to be a stranger who had heard much praise of the General Hospital, and of the order kept in it. I questioned him on the most minute details, and one thing leading to another, we arrived at the governors, on whose names and quality I begged to be informed. His answers on this last head inspired me with an idea on which I promptly congratulated myself, and lost no time in carrying out. I asked him, for it was essential to my design, if these gentlemen had children. He said that he could not tell me for certain about them all, but that there was M. de T . . . who was one of the principal governors; he knew that he had a son old enough to be married, who had come several times to the Hôpital with his Father. This was enough for me. Almost at once I broke off our conversation, and on our way back to the house, I confided to Lescaut the plan which I had formed. I imagine, said I, that the younger M. de T . . . who is rich and of good family, has the same taste for pleasure as most of the young men of his age. He could not be a woman-hater, nor so preposterous as to refuse his services in a love affair. I design to interest him in Manon's rescue. If he is a man of honour and of sensibility he will give us his help out of generosity. If he is not capable of being swayed by that motive, he will at least do something for a charming girl, if it were only in the hope of sharing her favours. I do not want to put off seeing him, I went on, further than to-morrow. I feel so comforted by this plan that it seems to me a good omen. Lescaut himself agreed that my idea was a likely one enough and that we might hope for something out of it. I passed that night less sorrowfully.

The morning come, I dressed myself as elegantly as my present state of poverty allowed, and took a cab to the house of M. de T . . . He was surprised to receive a visit from a stranger, but I augured well from his countenance and his courtesy. I found it easy to explain myself to him, and in order to kindle his natural sensibility,

I spoke of my passion and of my mistress's desert as two things which could find no match unless in each other. He told me that although he had never seen Manon, he had heard of her, at any rate if it were she who had been the Mistress of old G . . . M . . . I was certain that he had been told of my own share in that affair, and the better to engage him by a voluntary confidence, I told him in detail of all that had befallen Manon and me. You see, Sir, I went on, that my life and my heart are now in your hands. The one is no dearer to me than the other. I have had no reserve with you, because I am informed of your generosity, and the similarity in our ages gives me hope that there may be some in our inclinations. He seemed very sensible of this evidence of openness and candour. His reply was that of a man of the world, and of sensibilities which the world does not always give and which it sometimes banishes. He told me that he set my visit among his luckiest chances, that he would consider my friendship as one of his happiest acquisitions, and would endeavour to deserve it by the fervour of his services. He could not promise to restore me Manon, because he had only, he said, very moderate influence and indifferently assured; but he offered to procure me the pleasure of seeing her, and to do everything in his power to restore her to my arms. I was better satisfied with this uncertainty of his than I should have been with the fullest assurance of the fulfilment of my desires. I saw in the very moderation of his offers a sincerity and frankness which charmed me. I promised myself all the good offices he could bestow. His promise to let me see Manon would alone have made me attempt anything for him. I signified something of what I felt in a fashion which convinced him too that I was not ill-conditioned. We embraced with tenderness and became friends, for no other reason than the goodness of our hearts and the natural inclination which leads one sensitive and generous nature to love another like itself. He was to give me yet further proof of his regard: for after piecing together my adventures and judging that after escaping from Saint-Lazare I could not but be straitened in means, he offered me his purse and urged me to accept it. I did not accept it; but I did say: This is too much, my dear sir. If with all this goodness and friendliness you bring me to a sight of my dear Manon, I am yours for life. If you can restore me wholly to that beloved creature, I should not think myself out of your debt should I shed every drop of my blood in serving you.

We did not separate until we had agreed on the time and place of our next meeting. He had the goodness to postpone it no further than the afternoon of that same day. I waited for him in a café, where he came to join me about four o'clock, and we set out together towards the Hôpital. My knees were trembling as I crossed the courtyards. O power of love! said I, I am to see again the idol of my heart, the object of so many tears and distresses. Heaven! keep me in life until I reach her, and after that dispose as Thou wilt of my fortune and my days: I have no further boon to crave of Thee! M. de T . . . spoke to several of the concierges, who were eager to do all in their power to please him. He was shown the quarter where Manon had her room, and we were conducted thither, a key of terrifying size being used to open the door. I asked the man who guided us, and whose charge it was to wait upon her, how she had spent her time in that abode. He told us that she was of an angelic sweetness; that he had never had a harsh word from her: that she had been continually in tears for the first six weeks after her arrival, but that for some time she had seemed to be taking her ill-fortune with more patience, and that she busied herself in sewing from morning to night, except for some hours which she spent in reading. I asked him further if she had been properly fed. He had assured me that she had never lacked at any rate the necessities of life. We came near the door. My heart was beating violently. Go in alone, I said to M. de T . . ., and prepare her for my visit, for I fear that it might be too much for her to see me all at once. The door was opened to us. I stayed in the corridor. None the less I heard what they said. He told her that he had come to bring her a little consolation: that he was a friend of mine, and much concerned for my fortunes. She asked him with the utmost eagerness if he could tell her what had become of me. He promised her that he would bring me to her feet, as tender, as faithful as her heart could desire. When? said she. This very day, was his answer, that blessed moment will not be long in coming. He will appear this instant if you will have it so. She realised that I was at the door. I entered and she flung herself forward to meet me. We clung together with that overflowing tenderness which three months of absence makes ecstasy to perfect lovers. For a quarter of an hour our sighs, our broken exclamations, a thousand pet names murmured by one and by the other, made a scene that melted M. de T . . . I envy you, said he, making us sit down; there is no fate however glorious to which I should not prefer a mistress so lovely and so passionate. Even so would I scorn the empires of the world, was my answer, to secure the rapture of being loved by her.

The rest of a conversation so much desired could not fail to be infinitely tender. My poor Manon told me her adventures, and I recounted mine. We wept bitterly as we talked of the condition in which she was, and from which I had only just escaped. M. de T . . . comforted us by promising afresh to do his utmost to end our miseries. He advised us not to prolong this first interview unduly, so that it might be easier for him to procure us others. He had some difficulty in making us relish his advice. Manon especially could not bring herself to let me go. A hundred times she pulled me down upon my chair, she held me by the coat and by the hands. Alas! what place is this to leave me in! said she. How am I to know I shall see you again? M. de T . . . promised to come and see her often with me. As for the place, said he pleasantly, we must not call it the

Hôpital any more; it is Versailles, since a creature who deserves the empire of all hearts is here confined.

As I went out, I bestowed some bounties on the Valet who attended upon her, to ensure that he would wait on her with zeal. The fellow had a soul less base and less hardened than his like. He had been a witness of our meeting, and the sight had touched his heart. A louis d'or which I made him a present of, won him to me wholly. He took me aside as we went down to the courtyards. Sir, said he, if you would be willing to take me into your service or to give me what would make up to me for the loss of my situation here, I think that it would be easy for me to set Mademoiselle Manon free. I listened eagerly to his proposal, and though I was at the end of my resources, I made him promises far beyond his desires. I reckoned indeed that it would always be easy for me to recompense a man of his quality. Rest assured, my man, said I, that there is nothing I would not do for you, and that your fortune is as secure as my own. I was eager to learn what means he intended to employ. Nothing else, said he, but to open the door of her room some night, and take her down to you as far as the door into the street, where you would have to be ready to meet her. I asked him if there were no risk of her being recognised in passing through the corridors and the courtyards. He admitted that there was some danger of it; but one must, he said, risk something. Although I was enchanted to find him so resolute, I called M. de T . . . to tell him of the plan, and the sole reason which might make it doubtful. He saw more difficulty than I did. It was quite possible, he agreed, that she might escape in that way. But, he went on, if she is recognised and stopped in her flight, it is perhaps the end of her for ever. Besides, you would have to leave Paris at once, for you could never hide yourself from the hue and cry that will be made. Their efforts will be redoubled, as much on your behalf as hers. A man escapes easily enough when he is alone; but it is almost impossible to live unknown with a pretty woman. Solid as his reasoning appeared, it could not win the day in my mind against so instant a hope of setting Manon free. I said as much to M. de T . . ., and I prayed him to excuse a little rashness and temerity in love. I added that my intention was indeed to leave Paris and stay as I had already done, in some neighbouring village. We then agreed with the Attendant not to postpone his enterprise further than the following day: and to make it as certain as lay in our power, we determined to bring a man's suit of clothes, in order to facilitate the escape. It was not easy to have them brought in, but I did not lack ingenuity to devise some way. I only begged M. de T . . . to put on two light waist-coats, on the morrow, one on top of the other, and I undertook the rest. We returned in the morning to the Hôpital. I had brought linen, stockings, etc., for Manon, and on top of my coat an overcoat which kept my pockets from bulging too conspicuously. We were only a moment in her chamber. M. de T . . . left her one of his waistcoats, and I gave her my coat, the topcoat being enough for me to go out in; nothing was found lacking for her equipment, ex-cept the trousers which I had unluckily forgotten. The oversight of an article so essential would undoubtedly have set us all laughing, if the predicament it brought us had been less serious. I was in despair at being held up by a trifle of such a nature. However, I took my own measures, which were to go out trouserless myself. Mine I left to Manon. My topcoat was a long one, and with the help of a few pins, I put myself in case to get decently past the door. The rest of the day seemed insufferably long in passing. Night at last come, we drove to the Hôpital, and drew up the coach a little beyond the door. We had not long to wait till we saw Manon and her escort appear, our door was wide open, they lost no time in climbing in, I caught my dear mistress in my arms. She was trembling like a leaf. The coachman asked me where he was to drive us. Drive to the end of the world, said I, take me somewhere where I can never be parted from Manon.

It was a transport I could not have mastered, but it served to bring me into a vexatious plight. The coachman took note of my words: and on my finally telling him the name of the street to which we wished to be driven, he made answer that he was afraid I was mixing him up in an ugly bit of work: he could see for himself that this fine young man who called himself Manon was a wench I was carrying off from the Hôpital, and that he was in no notion of ruining himself out of love for me. The rascal's scruples were nothing but the hope of making me pay more for his carriage. We were too near the Hôpital not to pocket the affront. Hold your tongue, said I, there will be a louis d'or for you to earn. He would have helped me, after that, to burn down the Hôpital itself. We reached the house where Lescaut lived. As it was late, M. de T . . . had left us on the way, promising to see us again on the morrow. The Valet remained with us. I was holding Manon so close clasped in my arms that we filled only one seat in the coach. She was crying for joy, and I felt her tears wet on my face. But when the moment came to get down and go into Lescaut's house, I had a fresh altercation with the coachman, which was to have disastrous consequences. I repented having promised him a louis, not only because it was a preposterous sum, but for another and much stronger reason, which was my incapacity to pay it. I sent up for Lescaut. He came downstairs from his room and came to the door. I told him under my breath the predicament I was in. As he was rough in his ways, and not in the habit of humouring coachmen, he made answer that I was joking. A louis d'or! he added, a dozen well laid on with a cane for that sort of rascal. In vain did I urge upon him that he would be the ruin of us. He snatched my cane from me, as though about to use it on the coachman. The latter, whose fate it may sometimes have been to feel the hand of a Guardsman or a Musketeer, made off with his coach in alarm, shouting that I had cheated him, but that I should hear more of him. In vain I cried to him to stop. His flight caused me the most acute uneasiness. I had no doubt but that he would tell the Commissary. You have ruined us, said I to Lescaut. There would be no safety in staying with you: we must make off at once. I gave Manon my arm to start off on foot, and we at once made our way from that dangerous street. Lescaut came with us. There is something marvellous in the fashion in which Providence links up events. Scarcely had we been walking for more than five or six minutes when a man whose face I did not distinguish, recognised Lescaut. Undoubtedly he was lying in wait for him in the neighbourhood of his house, bent on the evil errand which he now carried out. 'Tis Lescaut! said he, firing a pistol at him, he will sup with the angels to-night. He made off at once. Lescaut fell, and never stirred: there was not the least flicker of life. I urged Manon to fly, for our aid was useless to a corpse, and I feared arrest by the Watch, who were bound soon to come on the scene. I made off down the first little cross street, with herself and the man-servant; she was so distraught, that I could hardly support her. At last, catching sight of a cab at the end of the street, I summoned it. We got in. But when the coachman asked me where he was to drive us, I was at a loss to answer him. I had no safe refuge, no trusty friend to whom I dared apply. I had no money: there was hardly more than half a pistole in my purse. Fright and fatigue had so affected Manon that she lay almost fainting against me. Moreover, my imagination was busy with the murder of Lescaut, and I did not yet feel secure from the watch. What course was I to take? Luckily I remembered the inn at Chaillot where I had spent some days with Manon, when we first went to live in that village. I had hopes not only of being safe there, but of being able to live for some time without being pressed for payment. To Chaillot, said I to the driver. He refused to go there so late, under a pistole: yet another embarrassment. At last we agreed on six francs. It was all I had in my purse.

I tried to comfort Manon as we drove: but in reality I had despair in my heart. I would have put an end to myself, were it not that I had in my arms the only thing that held me to life. That thought alone restored my self-command. I have her fast, at any rate, said I, she loves me, she is mine. Tiberge may talk as he likes: this is no phantom happiness. I could see the whole universe perish and pay no heed. Why? I care for naught else. The sentiment was genuine: and yet, even while I set so light by all the world's gifts, I felt that to have at least a fraction of them would have aided me to a still more sovereign scorn of all the rest. Love is stronger than wealth, stronger than riches or treasure, but it needs their aid; and nothing so disheartens a sensitive lover as to find himself dragged down thereby, in spite of himself, to the grossness of the coarsest souls. It was about eleven o'clock when we arrived at Chaillot. We were received at the inn as familiar guests. No one was surprised to see Manon in masculine dress, because in Paris and its neighbourhood people are accustomed to see women in all guises. I saw to it that she was attended as handsomely as if I had been at the height of my fortune. She did not know that I was badly off for money. I took good care to say nothing of it, resolving to return alone to Paris on the morrow and to seek some remedy for this distressing complaint. I thought her pale at supper, and thinner. I had not noticed it at the Hôpital, because the light in the room where I had seen her was not of the clearest. I asked her if it were not still the result of the fright she had had in seeing her brother murdered. She assured me that however distressed she had been by that accident, her pallor only came from having had to suffer three months of absence from me. Then you do love me, terribly? said I. A thousand times more than I can say, was her reply. And you will never leave me any more? I went on. No, never, she answered, and confirmed that assurance with so many endearments and vows that it seemed to me indeed impossible that she could ever forget them. I

*"I thought her pale at supper, and thinner. I asked her if it were not
still the result of the fright she had had"*

have always been convinced that she was sincere: what reason could she have had to dissemble to that degree? She was sincere, but she was fickle, or rather she ceased to be anything, she did not even recognise herself when she saw other women living in wealth before her eyes, and herself in poverty and want. I was on the eve of having a final proof of it, a proof that surpassed all the others and which brought about the strangest experience which could befall a man of my birth and fortune.

Knowing her disposition, I made haste on the morrow to go to Paris. Her brother's death, and the need we both were in of linen and clothes, were reasons enough without inventing excuses. I left the inn, saying both to Manon and my host, that I would take a hackney-coach: but that was bravado. Forced as I was to go on foot, I made good speed as far as Cours-la-Reine, where I had planned to halt. I must have a moment of solitude and tranquillity to compose myself and to determine what I was going to do in Paris. I sat down on the grass, and plunged into a sea of arguments and reflections, which finally reduced themselves gradually to three outstanding considerations. I had need of immediate help to meet an infinite number of immediate necessities. I had to seek some course that would at least open to me some prospects for the future; and, by no means least in importance, I had to get some information and take some steps to secure Manon's liberty and my own. After wearing myself out in plans and combinations to unite these three, I finally judged it best to cut out the last two. A room at Chaillot was tolerably good cover; and for future necessities, it would be time enough to think about them when I had satisfied the present. The question then was how actually to fill my purse. M. de T . . . had generously offered me his own: but the thought of putting myself on that footing was extremely repugnant to me. What part was this to play, to go and expose one's poverty to a stranger, and beg him to share his property with us? It is only a dastard who could be capable of it, thanks to the baseness that hinders him from feeling the indignity; or a humble Christian, by such an excess of nobility as makes him superior to shame. I was neither a dastard nor a good Christian: I would have shed half my blood to avoid such humiliation. Tiberge, said I, dear Tiberge, would he refuse me anything he had in his power to give me? No, he will be touched by my misery, but he will half-kill me with his moralising. I must endure his reproaches, his exhortations, his threats; he will make me buy his help so dear that I should shed still another half of my blood rather than face that wretched scene, that will leave me uneasy, and remorseful. Very well, I went on, there's nothing for it but to give up all hope, since I am left with no other course, and I am so far from fixing on these two that I would rather shed half my blood than take either of them, and my whole blood rather than take both. Yes, my whole blood, I added, after a moment's reflection; I would sooner give it than be degraded to this whining. But what has my blood got to do with it? What does matter is Manon's life and maintenance, Manon's love and faithfulness. Is there anything I would put in the scales against her? I have never done so until now, she takes the place with me of fame, of happiness, of fortune. There are plenty of things, no doubt, that I would give my life to obtain or to avoid: but to prize something as dearer than life is no reason for prizing it dearer than Manon. I was not long in coming to a resolution now. I took the road again, determined to go first to Tiberge, and then to M. de T . . .

Once in Paris, I took a cab, although I had not what would pay for it; I counted on the help I was going to beg for. I drove to the Luxembourg, whence I sent a message to Tiberge that I was there waiting for him. My impatience was satisfied by his prompt arrival. I told him of my extremity without any beating about the bush. He asked me if the hundred pistoles which I had given back to him would be enough; and without the least demurrer, he sent that instant to fetch them, with that frankness and pleasure in giving which is only to be found in love and in real friendship. Although I had never had any doubt of the success of my appeal, I was surprised at having obtained it so cheaply, without a word of complaint on my impenitence. But I was mistaken in thinking myself wholly quit of his reproaches; for when he had finished counting me out his money, and I was preparing to leave him, he begged me to take a turn with him down an alley. I had not spoken to him of Manon: he did not know that she was at liberty, consequently his moralising turned only upon my rash flight from Saint-Lazare, and his fear that instead of profiting by the lessons in wisdom that I had received there, I might fall again into dissolute ways. He told me that he had gone to visit me at Saint-Lazare the day after my escape, and had been aghast beyond all expression in hearing in what fashion I had left it; that he had had a talk with the Superior; that the good Father was not yet recovered from his fright, but that he had nevertheless been generous enough to conceal the circumstances of my escape from the Lieutenant-General of Police, and he had kept the death of the Porter from being known outside: that I had therefore nothing to fear on that account: but that if I had the least grain of wisdom left, I should profit by the happy turn which Heaven had given my affairs: that I should begin by writing to my father, and put myself on terms with him: and that if I would take his advice for once, he would counsel me to leave Paris and go back to the bosom of my family. I heard out his discourse to the end. A good deal of it was to my satisfaction. I was enchanted above all that I had nothing to fear from Saint-Lazare. The streets of Paris were a free country to me once again. In the second place, I congratulated myself that Tiberge had not the slightest idea of Manon's escape and her return to me. I even noted that he avoided mention of her, apparently in the idea that she had less sway in my heart, since I seemed so easy on that head. I resolved, if not to return to my family, at any rate to write to my father, as he advised, and assure him that I was willing to return to the path of duty and to follow his wishes. My hope was to induce him to send me money, on pretext of taking the courses at the Academy: for I should have difficulty in convincing him that I was minded to return to Holy Orders: and indeed I had no disinclination for the life I would propose to him. I was well content, on the contrary, to apply myself to some honourable and sensible pursuit, so long as this project could be reconciled with my love for Manon. I counted on being able to live with her, and at the same time to attend the course. The two things were compatible. So satisfied was I with all these ideas, that I promised Tiberge I would send off a letter to my father that very day. I did actually go into a stationer's, after leaving him, and wrote in so tender and submissive a tone as could not fail, I thought, to have some effect on my father's heart.

Although I was now in funds to take and pay for a cab, I felt it a pleasure to go boldly on foot. On my way to M. de T . . . I found delight in this exercise of my liberty, now that my friend had assured me it was not in danger. However, it all at once came into my mind that his assurances only related to Saint-Lazare, and that over and above that I had the affair of the Hôpital on my hands, not to speak of the death of Lescaut, in which I had been involved, if only as a witness. This thought so alarmed me, that I took to the first lane I saw, and then sent for a cab. I went straight to M. de T . . ., who fell to laughing at my alarm. It seemed ridiculous enough to myself when I learned from him that I had nothing to fear, neither as to the Hôpital, nor yet as to Lescaut. He said that, thinking he might be suspected of having a share in carrying off Manon, he had gone in the morning to the Hôpital, and had asked to see her, assuming ignorance of what had passed: so far were they from accusing us, either himself or me, that they were eager on the contrary to tell him the whole story as a bizarre piece of news, and were marvelling that so pretty a girl as Manon should have brought herself to run away with a Man-servant: he had contented himself with replying coldly that he was not surprised at it, and that people would do anything for freedom. He went on to tell me how he had gone to Lescaut's quarters, in the hope of finding me there with my charming mistress; that the landlord, who was a coachbuilder, protested that he had seen neither her nor me, but that it was no wonder we had not arrived at his house, if it were Lescaut we would have come to see, because we would doubtless have learned that he had just been killed about the time of which M. de T... spoke. Thereupon he recounted what he knew of the cause and circumstances of his death; he said that about two hours before a Guardsman, one of Lescaut's friends, had come to see him, and had suggested a game of cards; that Lescaut had won so rapidly that the other found himself poorer in less than an hour by a hundred crowns, which was all the money he had; that the poor wretch, left penniless, had begged Lescaut to lend him half the sum he had lost: they had words about it, and finally they fell to quarrelling most ferociously. Lescaut had refused to go out to settle it at the sword's point, and the other had left, vowing that he would break his head for him, which he would seem to have done that same night. M. de T... had the kindness to add that he had been very uneasy about us, and persisted in offering me his services. I did not hesitate to tell him the place of our retreat. He begged me to allow him to come to supper with us. As I had now nothing more to do but to buy linen and clothes for Manon, I told him that we could set off at once, if he would not mind my halting for a moment at various Merchants. I do not know if he thought that I suggested it in order to provoke his generosity, or if it were simply his own impulse, but, consenting to set off at once, he took me to the Merchants who supplied his own house; made me choose divers stuffs rather more costly than I had intended, and when I was about to pay, absolutely forbade the Merchant to take my money. He did me this courtesy with such a grace, that I felt I might take advantage of it without shame. Together we took the road to Chaillot, where I arrived in less disquiet than I had left it.

As more than an hour had now been spent by the Chevalier des Grieux in telling his story, I begged him to take a rest till we had our supper. He confessed that he himself would be glad of it and judging by our attention that we had heard his story with pleasure, he assured us that we would find the rest of it more interesting still. When supper was over, he resumed as follows.

Book II

MY PRESENCE and the company of M. de T . . . soon put to
flight any traces of distress in Manon. Let's forget all our
past fears, dearest love, said I, as I came in, and begin to live again,
happier than ever. After all, Love is a kind master. Fate could not
cause us as much pain as he has given us of pleasure. The supper
was a veritable scene of joy. I was prouder and more content with
Manon and my hundred pistoles than the richest Citizen in Paris
with his heaps of gold. Riches are to be reckoned by the means one
has of satisfying one's desires: I had not one left unfulfilled. Even
the future caused me no uneasiness. I was almost certain that my
father would make no difficulties in giving me enough to live like a
gentleman in Paris, since being in my twentieth year, I had a right
to demand my share of my mother's estate. I did not conceal from
Manon that the amount of my wealth was no more than a hundred
pistoles. It was enough on which to await better fortune with an
easy mind, and that it seemed I could not fail of, either from my
family or from the gaming table.

I have observed throughout my whole life that Heaven has
always chosen to strike me with its harshest chastisement at that
moment when my fortune seemed most securely founded. I thought
myself so happy, supping with M. de T . . . and Manon, that no one
could have made me believe I had a fresh obstacle to my happiness
yet to fear; yet one was in preparation, so sinister that it reduced me
to the state in which you saw me at Passy, and finally to extremities

so pitiable that you will hardly be able to believe my tale is true. While we were at table, we heard the sound of a coach stopping at the door of the Inn. Curiosity made us wish to know who it might be arriving so late. We were told that it was the young G . . . M . . ., that is to say the son of our most cruel enemy, the old profligate who had sent me to Saint-Lazare and Manon to the Hôpital. His name brought the blood to my face. It is Heaven who brings him to me, said I to M. de T . . ., to punish him for his father's baseness. He shall not escape me till we have measured our swords. M. de T . . ., who knew him and who was even one of his best friends, tried to bring me to a better mind upon him. He assured me that he was a very amiable young man, so incapable of having had any share in his father's action, that I myself could not see him for a moment without giving him my regard and desiring his own. After adding a thousand things to his credit, he begged me to agree to his going to him and proposing that he should sit down with us and share the rest of our supper. He forestalled objection as to the peril to Manon in betraying her whereabouts to the son of our enemy, by protesting on his word of honour that let him once know us and we should have no more zealous champion. I made no difficulty of any kind, after such assurances. M. de T . . . brought him to us after taking a moment to tell him who we were. He entered with an air which prejudiced us at once in his favour. He embraced me and we sat down. He admired Manon, myself, everything about us, and he ate with an appetite that did honour to our supper. The table cleared, the conversation took a more serious turn. He spoke with abhorrence of the extremes to which his father's wrath against us had borne him, and made us the humblest apologies. I cut them short, said he, so as not to revive a memory which causes me too much humiliation. If they were sincere at the outset, they became much more so as time passed; for he had not spent half an hour in conversing with us when I observed the impression which Manon's charms were making upon him. I saw his gaze and his manner become gradually more tender. He let nothing of it escape in his conversation; but without the aid of jealousy I had too much experience in love not to recognise whatever derives from that spring. He kept us company during part of the night, and only left us after congratulating himself on our acquaintance, and begging us to grant him permission to come again sometime to renew the offer of his services. He set off in the morning with M. de T . . ., who took a seat in his coach.

I never had, as I have said, any inclination to jealousy. I was more credulous than ever of Manon's vows. That charming creature was so absolute mistress of my soul that I had not a single passing thought of her that was not esteem and love. Far from blaming her for having been found pleasing by G . . . M . . ., I was enchanted by this proof of her charm, and I congratulated myself on being loved by a girl whom everyone found lovable. I did not even think fit to tell her the suspicion I had conceived of G . . . M . . . We were occupied for a few days with the business of having her clothes fitted, and in discussing whether we might go to the Comédie without fear of being recognised. M. de T . . . came back to see us before the end of the week; we consulted him upon it. He saw that if he was to please Manon he must say yes. We decided to go with him that very evening, a resolution however which was not to be carried out: for he at once drew me to one side. I have been in the utmost embarrassment since I saw you, said he, and my coming here to-day is a result of it. G . . . M . . . is in love with your mistress; he has made me his confidant. I am his intimate friend, and ready to serve him in anything: but I am none the less yours. To my mind, his intentions are unjustifiable, and I have condemned them. Nevertheless, I should have kept his secret if he had only meant to use the ordinary ways of commending himself: but he is well aware of Manon's disposition. He has learned, I know not where, that she loves luxury and diversion, and as he already owns a good deal of property, he declares that he means to tempt her first by a very handsome present, and the offer of an allowance of £10,000. Other things being equal, I should have had to do a good deal more violence to myself before betraying him to you, but in your case justice reinforces friendship, all the more that since I was the thoughtless cause of his passion by introducing him here, I am bound to prevent the consequences of the evil I brought about.

I thanked M. de T . . . for a service of such importance, and I admitted to him, in frank return for his confidence, that Manon's character was even as G . . . M . . . had imagined, that is, that she could not endure the thought of poverty. All the same, I went on, when it is only a question of more or less, I do not believe her capable of abandoning me for another. I am in a position to let her want for nothing, and I count on my fortune increasing every day. I fear only one thing, I added, that G . . . M . . . will use the knowledge he has of our whereabouts to do us some ill turn. M. de T . . . assured me that I need be under no apprehension on that head: that G . . . M . . . was capable of a lover's folly, but not of actual baseness: that if he were dastardly enough to commit such an act, he, the speaker, would be the first to avenge it, and make amends thereby for the harm of which he had been the occasion. I am obliged to you for feeling thus, said I, but the mischief would be done, and the remedy very uncertain. The wisest course therefore is to forestall it, by leaving Chaillot and finding some other abode. True, replied M. de T . . ., but you will have trouble in doing so as soon as needs be, for G . . . M . . . is to be here at noon: he told me so yesterday, and that is what brought me here so early, to warn you of his intentions. He may be here at any moment. This last circumstance made me take the whole affair more seriously. As it seemed impossible to avoid the visit of G . . . M . . . and doubtless equally so to keep him from declaring himself to Manon, I deter-

mined on warning her myself as to the design of this new Rival.
I imagined that knowing me already informed of the proposals
which he would make her, and receiving them under my eye, she
would have enough strength of mind to reject them and remain
faithful to me. I confided my plan to M. de T . . ., who made answer
that it was a very delicate business. I admit it, said I, but if ever
lover had grounds to be secure of a mistress's heart, I have to count
on the love of mine. There's nothing here but the magnificence of
his offers to dazzle her, and I have told you that she cares nothing
for money. She loves her ease, but she loves me too: and in the
present state of my affairs, I could not believe that she would prefer
to me the son of a man who sent her to the Hôpital. To be brief,
I persisted in my plan, and taking Manon apart, I told her straight-
forwardly all that I had just learned. She thanked me for the good
opinion I had of her, and promised me to receive the proposals of
G . . . M . . . in such a fashion as would leave the young man small
inclination to renew them. Not so, said I, you must not irritate him
by an affront: he can do us an ill turn; but you know very well, all
you rascals, I added with a laugh, how to get rid of a disagreeable
or tiresome suitor. She reflected a little. A wonderful plan has just
come into my head, said she, and I am very vain of having thought
of it. G . . . M . . . is the son of our bitterest enemy; we must
avenge ourselves of the father, not upon the son, but upon his
purse. I am going to listen to him, accept his presents, and make a
fool of him. A very pretty plan, said I, but you forget, my poor
child, that that was the road that took us straight to the Hôpital.
But in vain did I point out to her the danger of such an enterprise.
She told me that it all depended on our precautions, and she
countered every one of my objections. Show me the Lover who
does not enter blindfold into every whim of an adored mistress, and I shall agree that I was wrong in yielding so readily
to mine. It was resolved to make a dupe of G . . . M . . ., and

by a fantastic trick of fate, it happened that I was to become his.

Towards eleven o'clock we saw his coach arriving. He made us very handsome excuses for the liberty he took in coming to dine with us. He was not surprised to see M. de T . . ., who had promised him the day before to be here, and who had invented a plea of business to avoid coming in the same coach. Although there was not one of us but had treason in his heart, we sat down to table with an air of friendly confidence. G . . . M . . . easily found an opportunity to declare himself to Manon; he could not have found me in the way, for I absented myself for several minutes on purpose. I observed, on my return, that he had not been driven to despair by any excessive rigour. He was in the best possible humour. I pretended likewise; he was laughing inwardly at my simplicity, and I at his; throughout the whole afternoon, each staged for the other a most agreeable comedy. I again engineered him, before his departure, a moment of private talk with Manon, so that he had reason to congratulate himself on my good nature as well as on my good cheer. As soon as he had got into the coach beside M. de T . . ., Manon ran to me open armed, and kissed me, with peals of laughter. She recited me his speeches and his proposals without altering a word. They came to this: he adored her: he would share with her the income of forty thousand *livres* which he already enjoyed, not counting his expectations after the death of his father. She would be mistress of his heart and his purse; and by way of overture to his benefactions, he was prepared to give her a coach, a furnished house, a lady's maid, two footmen, and a cook. There's a son for you, said I, a deal more generous than his father. But in good faith, tell me now, I added, does this offer not tempt you at all? I? she replied, adapting to her thought these lines from Racine:

> I! you suspect me of this perfidy?
> I! could I then endure that odious face
> That brings the Hôpital before my eyes?

No, I replied, keeping up the parody.

> I hardly think the Hôpital, Madame,
> Is like to grave his image in your Soul.

But there is something very seductive about a furnished house, and a carriage and three lackeys, and love has few advantages so solid. She protested that her heart was mine for ever, and that it would never receive any image but mine. The promises he has made me, said she, will be spurs to vengeance rather than shafts of love. I asked her if she was minded to accept the house and the carriage. She made answer that she had no mind to anything but the money. The difficulty was to obtain the one without the other. We resolved to await the final unfolding of G . . . M . . .'s plan, in a letter which he had promised to write her. This indeed she received the next day by a lackey not in livery, who very cleverly made an opportunity of speaking to her without witnesses. She bade him wait for her answer, and came at once to bring me the letter. We opened it together. In addition to the ordinary commonplaces of tenderness, it contained a detailed account of my Rival's promises. He was prepared for unlimited expenditure. He pledged himself to hand her ten thousand francs cash down when she took possession of the house, and to make good all diminutions of that sum, so that she would always have it to depend on as ready money. The day of inauguration was not too remote. He asked but two days in which to order things for her reception, and he told her the name of the street and the house, where he promised to be waiting for her on the afternoon of the second day, if she could manage to slip out of my hands. This was the only point on which he begged her to reassure his uneasiness; of the rest he seemed secure: but he added that if she foresaw any difficulty in escaping from me, he would find means to facilitate her flight.

G . . . M . . . had more guile than his father. He wanted to be sure of his prey before counting out the coin. We deliberated as the course of conduct Manon had better take. Once again I tried to persuade her to put the enterprise out of her head, and pointed out all its risks. She was bent on going through with the adventure. She wrote a brief reply to G . . . M . . ., reassuring him that nothing would be easier than for her to betake herself to Paris on the appointed day, and that he might expect her without fail. We then agreed that I should set out at once to rent a new lodging in some village on the other side of Paris, and that I should take our scanty baggage along with me: that in the afternoon of the next day, which was that of her assignation, she should appear in good time in Paris: that after receiving G . . . M . . .'s presents she should coax him to take her to the Comédie, should take with her as much money as she could carry, and entrust the rest to my Man-servant, whom she meant to take with her. It was he who had rescued her from the Hôpital, and he was infinitely attached to us. I was to arrive in a cab at the entrance to the Rue Saint-André-des-Arts, leave it there about seven o'clock, and myself come forward into the shadow at the door of the Comédie; Manon promised that she would invent some excuse to leave her box for a moment, and would use it to slip downstairs to join me; to carry out the rest would be easy. In a moment we would have regained the cab, and would be leaving Paris by the Faubourg Saint-Antoine, which was the road to our new abode. This plan, extravagant as it was, seemed to us tolerably well devised; but there was at bottom a kind of insane rashness in imagining that however happily it might succeed, we could ever be able to hide ourselves from its consequences. We took the risks, however, with the most reckless confidence. Manon set off with Marcel, as our manservant was called. I saw her go with grief. Manon, said I as I held her in my arms, you are not deceiving me? You will be faithful to me? She chided me tenderly for my mistrust, and reiterated all her vows. She reckoned on arriving in

Paris towards three o'clock. I set out after her, and went to eat my heart out for the rest of the afternoon in the Café de Feré, on the Pont Saint-Michel. There I stayed till six. I then went out to take a cab, which I posted according to our plan at the entrance to the Rue Saint-André-des-Arts: and thence came on foot to the door of the Comédie. I was surprised not to find Marcel, who was to have been waiting for me there. I mustered up patience to wait for an hour, unnoticed in a crowd of lackeys, intent on everyone who came or went. At length, when seven o'clock had struck, and I had seen nothing that had to do with our plan, I took a ticket for the parterre, to see if I could discover Manon and G . . . M . . . in the boxes. Neither was there. I returned to the door, where I passed yet another quarter of an hour, beside myself with impatience and anxiety. Then, having still seen nothing, I went back to my cab, helpless to decide on any course. The coachman, catching sight of me, came a few steps to meet me, and told me under his breath that there was a young lady in the carriage who had been waiting for me for an hour: that she had asked for me, describing me so that he had easily recognised me, and on learning that I was to come back, she had said that she would not mind waiting for me. I at once imagined that it was Manon. I came up, but I saw a pretty little face that was not hers. It was a stranger, who began by asking me if she had not the honour of speaking to the Chevalier des Grieux? I told her that such was my name. I have a letter to give you, she continued, which will tell you what it is that brings me here, and how I come to know your name. I begged her to give me time to read it in a neighbouring tavern. She was anxious to follow me, and advised me to ask for a private room. Who sent this letter? said I, going upstairs. She put me off till I should read it.

I recognised Manon's handwriting; this is roughly the tenor of it. G . . . M . . . had received her with a courtesy and a magnificence beyond all her dreams. He had overwhelmed her with presents, and he pictured for her the lot of a Queen. None the less she assured me that she had not forgotten me in this novel splendour, but since she could not persuade G . . . M . . . to take her that evening to the Comédie, she postponed the pleasure of seeing me till another day; and to console me a little for the pain which she foresaw this news would cost me, she had found means to provide me with one of the prettiest girls in Paris, who would be the Bearer of her note. Signed: Your faithful love, Manon Lescaut.

There was something so cruel and so insulting to me in this letter, that, suspended for some time between wrath and grief, I determined to make an effort to forget for ever my forsworn and thankless mistress. I cast my eyes upon the girl beside me. She was excessively pretty, and I could have wished that she were sufficiently so to make me forsworn and faithless in my turn: but I failed to find there those lovely wistful eyes, that heavenly carriage, that complexion of love's own blending, that inexhaustible depth of charm which nature had lavished on my faithless Manon. No, no, said I, turning away my gaze, the thankless heart that sent you knew too well that it was on a fruitless errand. Go back to her and tell her from me that she may enjoy at her ease her crime, enjoy it, if she can, without remorse; I give her up for ever; and, at the same time I renounce all women, who can never be as lovable as she, and who doubtless are as base, as false of faith. I was just about to go downstairs and take myself off, with never a thought of further claim to Manon; and the mortal jealousy which was rending my heart disguising itself in a sullen and dark tranquillity, I believed myself all the nearer to my final cure that I felt none of those violent emotions with which I had been shaken on the former occasions. Alas! I was as much the dupe of love, as I felt myself to be of G . . . M . . . and of Manon. The young woman who had brought me the letter, seeing me about to go downstairs, asked me what I would have her tell Monsieur G . . . M . . . and the lady who was

with him. At this question I came back into the room; and in a revulsion of feeling incredible to those who have never felt a violent
passion, I suddenly found myself, in lieu of the tranquillity I had
believed mine, in a terrible transport of anger. Go, said I, tell that
traitor G . . . M . . . and his false mistress the despair into which
your accursed letter has hurled me; but let them know that they
will not have long to laugh at it; and that I shall stab them both
with my own hand. I flung myself down on a chair. My hat fell to
one side, my cane to the other. Torrents of bitter tears began to
flow from my eyes. The fury which I had just felt changed into a
profound grief. I could only weep, uttering groans and sighs. Come
here, child, come here! I cried to the young girl, since it is you they
have sent to comfort me. Tell me if you can what comfort there is
against rage and despair, against the wish to put an end to one's self,
after killing two traitors who do not deserve to live. Yes, come
here, I went on, seeing her make a few timid and uncertain steps
towards me, come, and dry my tears: come and give peace again to
my heart; come and tell me that you love me, so that I may grow
used to being loved by another than my false one. You are fair; I
may perhaps be able to love you in my turn. The poor child who
was not more than sixteen or seventeen, and who seemed to have
more modesty than her kind, was surprised out of measure at so
strange a scene. She drew near, however, to offer me a few caresses;
but I brushed her at once aside, thrusting her off with my hands. What
do you want with me? said I. Ah, you are a woman; you belong to
a sex I detest, and which I can endure no longer. The sweetness of
your face bodes me some fresh treason. Be off, and leave me here
alone. She dropped me a curtsey without daring to speak to me,
and turned to go out. I cried to her to stop. But tell me at least, said
I, why, how, and for what purpose you were sent here? How did
you find out my name and the place where you could find me? She
told me that she had known M. de G . . . M . . . this great while:

that he had sent for her at five o'clock, and following the lackey who had come to fetch her, she had gone into a great house, where she had found him playing piquet with a pretty lady, and that they had both charged her to deliver me the letter she had brought me, and told her that she would find me in a coach at the end of the Rue Saint-André. I asked her if they had said nothing else, she answered with a blush that they had given her hope that I would take her to keep me company. They cheated you, my poor girl, said I, they cheated you. You are a woman, you must have a man: but it must be one who is rich and happy, and it is not here you will find him. Go back, go back to M. de G . . . M . . .: he has everything that a man must have to be loved by pretty women, he has establishments and carriages to give away; as for me, who have only love to offer, women despise my poverty, and make sport of my simplicity.

I added a thousand things, sorrowful or violent, according as the passions that shook me yielded or seized the mastery in turn; however, by dint of my own torture, my frenzies abated sufficiently to give room to reflection. I compared this last misfortune with those of the same kind which I had already suffered, and I found it no more irretrievable than its predecessors. I knew Manon: why distress myself so for a misfortune which I ought to have foreseen? Why not rather busy myself in seeking out a remedy? There was still time. At least I must spare no pains if I did not wish to have myself to blame for having contributed to my own sufferings by my negligence. Thereupon I set myself to consider all the means that might open me a door to hope.

To attempt to tear her by main force from the hands of G . . . M . . . was a counsel of desperation that could only end in my ruin, and promised not even the semblance of success; but it seemed to me that if I could procure even the briefest interview with her, I should infallibly have some power upon her heart. I knew so well where it could be touched! I was so sure she loved me! Even this preposterous idea of sending me a pretty girl to comfort me, I could have sworn it was of her invention, and prompted by her love and pity for my sufferings. I resolved to use all my ingenuity to see her. Amid various devices which I reviewed one after the other, I settled upon this. M. de T . . . had already stood me in stead with too much affection for me to have the slightest doubt of his sincerity and zeal. I proposed to go to him there and then, and beg him to send for G . . . M . . . under colour of urgent business. I must have half an hour to speak with Manon. My plan was to have myself admitted into her very chamber, and I believed I should find it easy, once G . . . M . . . were absent. This determination bringing me some ease of mind, I gave a generous sum to the young woman, who was still with me, and in order that she might have no wish to go back to those who had sent her to me, I took her address, meanwhile giving her to hope that I was going to spend the night with her. I got into my cab, and was driven at full speed to the house of M. de T . . . I had the good fortune to find him at home: the thought had given me some uneasiness on the way. He was soon in possession of my trouble and the service I had come to ask of him. So astonished was he to learn that G . . . M . . . had succeeded in seducing Manon, unaware as he was that I had had some share in my own misfortune, that he generously offered to gather all his friends and set to with arms and sword to rescue my mistress. I made him see that such a hurly-burly might be disastrous for Manon and for me. Let us keep bloodshed for the last resort, said I. I have in mind a milder course, and one from which I hope no less success. He pledged himself, without reservation, to do whatever I might ask of him. I assured him that all that was required was to send word to G . . . M . . . that he had occasion to speak with him, and to keep him out for an hour or two. He set off with me there and then to carry out my plan. On our way, we cast about for some expedient that might serve to keep him away for that length of time. I advised him to write at first a simple note, dated from a tavern and begging him to come at once on a matter so pressing that it brooked no delay. I shall watch, said I, for the moment he goes out, and shall easily manage to get into the house, since no one in it knows me except Manon, and Marcel, my own Valet. As for you, who will by that time be with G . . . M . . ., you can tell him that the pressing business on which you wished to see him is need of cash: that you have just lost all you have at cards, and had gone on playing on your word with the same ill luck. It will take him some time to go with you to his strong-box, and that will give me long enough to carry out my design.

M. de T . . . carried out this scheme from point to point. I left him in a tavern, where he promptly wrote his letter, and went to post myself a few paces from Manon's house. I saw the bearer of the message arrive, and G . . . M . . . go out a moment later, followed by a lackey. After giving him time to be clear of the street, I made my way to the door of my false love, and in spite of all my anger, I knocked with the respect that one feels for a shrine. Happily it was Marcel who came to open. I signed to him to hold his tongue, and in an under-tone, though I had nothing to fear from the other servants, I asked him if he could bring me to the room where Manon was without my being seen. That he said was easy: I had only to go quietly up the grand staircase. Quick, then, said I, and while I am there, try to prevent anyone from coming up. I made my way without hindrance to the apartment. Manon was busy reading. And here I had cause to marvel at the character of this strange girl. Far from being terrified or seeming timid at the sight of me, she showed only those trifling signs of surprise which escape one at sight of a person one believes far distant. Ah, 'tis you, my love, said she, coming to embrace me with her usual tenderness. Lord, how bold you are! who would have expected to see you here today! I disengaged myself from her arms, and far from returning her caresses, I repulsed her with scorn, and stepped back two or three paces to keep my distance from her. This movement did not fail to disconcert her. She remained as she was, and, changing colour, she lifted her eyes to mine. I was at bottom so overjoyed at seeing her again, that with so many just causes for anger, I could hardly open my lips to reproach her. Yet my heart was bleeding at the cruel outrage she had done me; I recalled it vividly to my memory so as to revive my scorn, and I tried to bring another blaze to my eyes than that of love. For some time I stood in silence, and she realised my agitation. Then I saw her trembling, as though in fear.

I could not bear that sight. Ah Manon, said I tenderly, faithless, forsworn Manon! where shall I begin to make my plaint? I see you white and trembling, and I am still so stirred by your slightest pain that I fear to hurt you overmuch by my reproaches. But, Manon, you have pierced my heart, I tell you, with grief at your treachery. There are some blows one only gives a lover when one is set on his death. This is the third time, Manon, I have counted them well: there is no forgetting that. It is for you to consider this very hour what course you mean to take, for my sad heart can bear this cruel strain no longer. I feel it flagging, and nigh to break with grief. I can do no more, I added, sinking on a chair, I have hardly strength enough to speak or stand. She made no answer: but when I had sat down, she slipped to her knees, and leant her head on my lap, hiding her face in my hands. In a moment, I felt them wet with her tears. Oh God! how was my heart torn! Ah, Manon, Manon, I began, with a sigh, it is late to give me tears, when you have caused my death. You pretend a sadness that you cannot feel. That I am here is doubtless the greatest of your troubles: I have always stood in the way of your pleasures. Open your eyes, see who I am: one does not shed such tender tears for a wretch one has betrayed and abandoned. She was kissing my hands, without changing her position. Inconstant Manon, I went on, thankless and faithless, where

are your promises and your vows? O love, a thousandfold fickle and unkind, what have you done with the love that you swore to me again to-day? Just Heaven! said I, shall a faithless heart thus mock Thee, after calling Thee so piously to witness? So it is perjury that is rewarded! Despair and desolation are for constancy and faith!

These words were spoken from a conviction so bitter that in spite of myself some tears escaped me. Manon became aware of them by the change in my voice. At last she broke the silence. I must be in fault, said she sadly, since I have caused you so much pain and grief: but may Heaven punish me if I ever thought I was, or if I ever meant to be! This speech seemed to me so utterly devoid of sense or of good faith, that I could not refrain from a swift burst of wrath. O horrible dissembling! I cried. Now, better than ever, do I see you, what you are, a jade and a trickster. Now, now I know your vileness. Farewell, base creature, I went on, rising to my feet, rather would I die a thousand times than have henceforth the slightest commerce with you. May Heaven punish myself if I ever honour you with the least glance again. Live with your new Lover, love him, hate me, renounce all honour and all feeling: I can laugh now, 'tis all one to me. So appalled was she by my frenzy that, still on her knees beside the chair from which I had risen, she gazed at me, trembling, hardly daring to breathe. I took some further steps towards the door, my head turned, my eyes still fixed upon her. But I must needs have lost every sentiment of humanity if I could have hardened my heart against such charm. So far was I from having that savage strength, that, passing to the other extreme, I came back, or rather plunged back without a thought. I took her in my arms, I gave her a thousand tender kisses, I asked her pardon for my madness. I confessed that I was a brute, that I did not deserve the happiness of being loved by such a girl. I made her sit down, and, myself this time on my knees, I

conjured her to listen to me. There, whatever a humble and passionate lover could devise of respectful tenderness, I put into my pleading. I begged her in mercy to say that she forgave me. She let fall her arms about my neck, saying that it was she who had need of my goodness if I were to be made forget the grief she had caused me, and that she began to fear that I would not relish what she had to say to me in her own excuse. To me! I broke in. Ah, I ask for no excuses from you: I approve of everything you have done. It is not for me to demand your reasons for this or that. Too content, too happy, if my beloved does not deny me her tenderness. But, I went on, recalling to mind my immediate fate, all powerful Manon! you who have at your pleasure my sorrows and my joys, when I have satisfied you with my humiliation and the proofs of my repentance, will it not be allowed me to speak to you of my sadness and my griefs? Am I to learn from you what is to become of me this day, and if it is without reprieve that you are going to sign my death warrant, by spending the night with my Rival?

She was some time thinking out her reply. My Chevalier, said she, recovering her tranquil look, if you had explained yourself so clearly at the first, you would have spared yourself a good deal of misery, and me a distressing scene. Since it was only jealousy that made you wretched, I would have cured you by offering to follow you that moment to the ends of the earth. But I thought it was the letter that I wrote you under the eyes of M. de G . . . M . . ., and the girl that he sent you that had upset you. I thought you might have taken the letter as a mock, and the girl, coming to you as you might think on my behalf, as a declaration that I was giving up everything to attach myself to G . . . M . . . It was that thought that threw me into such consternation, for no matter how innocent I was, I could see when I thought about it, that appearances did not look well for me. But, she went on, I would have you be my judge, once I have told you the truth of it. She then told me all that had happened to her since she found G . . . M . . . waiting for her where we now were. He had indeed received her as if she were the first Princess of the world. He had shown her all the apartments, which were in admirable taste and elegance. In his cabinet he had counted out to her ten thousand pounds, and had added thereto several trinkets, among which were the pearl necklace and bracelets she had already had from his father; then he had brought her into a salon which she had not yet seen, where she found an exquisite repast. He had her waited on by the new servants he had hired for her, bidding them regard her henceforth as their mistress: finally he had shown her the carriage, the horses, and all the rest of his presents: and finally had proposed a game of cards while waiting for supper. I must confess, she went on, that I was struck by all this magnificence. I thought to myself that it would be a pity if we were to lose so many fine things all at once, supposing I should content myself by carrying off only the 10,000 francs and the jewels: there was our fortune made for you and me, and we could live very pleasantly at G . . . M . . .'s expense. Instead of suggesting going to the Comédie, it came into my head to sound him about you, so as to be able to guess what chance we should have of seeing each other if my way of it were carried out. I found him very easy to handle. He asked me what I thought of you, and if I had not had some regrets in leaving you. I said that you were so amiable and had always treated me so honourably that it would not be in nature for me to hate you. He admitted that you had merit, and that he had felt drawn to desire your friendship. He wanted to know how I thought you would take my departure, above all when you would come to know that I was in his hands. I told him that our love was of such long standing that it had had time to cool a little; that, besides, you were not too well off, and that perhaps you would not look on the loss of me as any great misfortune, since it would rid you of a burden that was heavy on your hands. I added that I was so convinced you

would take it peaceably that I had made no difficulty about telling you that I was coming to Paris for some commissions; that you had agreed, had come along yourself, and had not seemed particularly uneasy when I left you. If I thought, said he, that he would be disposed to be on good terms with me, I should be the first to offer him my services and my compliments. I assured him that from what I knew of you, I did not doubt but you would meet him frankly, above all, I said, if he could be any service to you in your affairs, which were a good deal disordered, thanks to your being on bad terms with your family. He broke in to protest that he would do you whatever service lay in his power, and that if you were minded even to embark on another love affair, he would procure you a pretty mistress, whom he himself had given up to devote himself to me. I applauded this idea, she added, the better to disarm any suspicion: and becoming more and more set on my plan, my only wish was to find some way of telling you about it, for fear you should be too much alarmed when you found that I failed to keep our assignation. It was for this reason that I proposed he should send you this new mistress that very evening, so that I might have an opportunity to write to you; I had to have recourse to that artifice, because I could not hope that he would leave me alone for a moment. My proposal made him laugh. He called his lackey, asked him if he could find his former mistress there and then, and sent him this way and that to look for her. He imagined that she would have to go to Chaillot to find you, but I told him that on leaving you I had promised to meet you at the Comédie, or that if anything prevented me, you were to wait for me in a carriage at the end of the Rue Saint-André; so that it would do better to send your new sweetheart to you there, if it were only to keep you from shivering there all night. I said too that it would be well to write you a line to explain the exchange, which you would hardly otherwise understand. He agreed; but I had to write it in his presence,

and I was very careful not to explain myself too openly in my letter. There, said Manon, now you see how it happened. I am not hiding anything from you, either what I did, or what I meant to do. The young girl came, I thought her pretty, and as I was very sure that you would suffer from my absence, I did sincerely hope that she might serve to beguile some dreary moments, for the fidelity I want from you is the fidelity of the heart. I would have been delighted if I could have sent you Marcel; but I could not get him to myself for a moment to explain to him what I wanted to let you know. She ended her story by describing the perplexity in which G . . . M . . . found himself on receiving the note from M. de T . . . He hesitated, said she, if he ought to leave me, and assured me that he would not delay his return: that is why I cannot but be anxious at seeing you here, and why I showed surprise when you came.

I listened to this story with a good deal of patience. I saw indeed plenty of cruel and mortifying features in it; for the intention to be unfaithful to me was so plain, that she had not even troubled to disguise it from me. She could not hope that G . . . M . . . would leave her all night like a vestal virgin. So then she had reckoned on spending it with him. What a confession to make to a lover! Yet I called to mind that I was partly to blame for her fault, by first letting her know of G . . . M . . .'s feelings towards her, and by my compliance in entering blindly into the madness of her adventure. Besides, by an odd twist of sympathy which is peculiar to me, I was touched by the ingenuousness of her story, and her simple open way of telling even those circumstances which outraged me most. She sins without malice, I said to myself; she is fickle and rash, but she is straightforward and sincere. Add that love alone was enough to close my eyes to all her faults. I was only too content with the hope of carrying her off that very night from my Rival. I said to her, however, And to-night, with whom would you have spent it? That question which I put to her sadly enough, embarrassed her.

She only answered me by broken *Buts* and *ifs*. I took pity on her distress, and breaking off, I told her simply that I expected her to follow me that very hour. I will, gladly, said she, but do you not think well of my plan? Ah! is it not enough, I retorted, that I think well of everything you have done up till now? What! not carry off even the ten thousand francs? she replied. He has given them to me; they belong to me. I advised her to leave everything behind, and only think of getting quickly away, for although I had been with her barely half an hour, I feared that G . . . M . . . might return. However, she was so instant with me to get my consent not to go away empty-handed, that I felt I must concede something, after obtaining so much.

Whilst we were making ready for departure, I heard a knock at the street door. I never dreamt but that it was G . . . M . . ., and in the revulsion caused by that thought I told Manon that he was a dead man if he appeared. In very truth I had not come to myself sufficiently after my outburst to control myself at sight of him. Marcel put me out of my pain by bringing to me a note which had been given him for me at the door. It was from M. de T . . . It informed me that as G . . . M . . . was gone to his house in quest of funds for him, he took advantage of his absence to share with me a happy thought; that to his mind I could not more agreeably revenge myself upon my Rival than by eating his supper, and lying that very night in the bed which he had meant to occupy along with my mistress; that this might, he thought, easily be done, if I could secure three or four men who would have courage enough to stop him in the street, and fidelity enough to keep him in sight till the morning; that for his own part, he would undertake to keep him amused for another hour at least by various plans which he held in readiness against his return. I showed this note to Manon, and told her the ruse by which I had managed to introduce myself into her house. My own contrivance and this of M. de T . . . delighted her,

we made merry over it for a moment or two, but when I spoke of
the letter as a pleasantry, I was astonished to find her serious in
urging it upon me as a plan that must be carried out. In vain I
asked her where she thought I would there and then find men fit to
arrest G . . . M . . . and keep him close: she said that we must at
least try, since M. de T . . . guaranteed us still another hour, and in
reply to my other objections, she told me that I was playing the
tyrant and would do nothing to please her. It was the prettiest plan
in the world. You will have his place at supper, she repeated, you
will lie in his sheets, and to-morrow morning early you will carry
off his mistress and his money. You will be thoroughly revenged on
both father and son. I yielded to her insistence, in spite of the secret
rebelling of my heart, which seemed to forebode some catastrophe.
I went out, intending to ask two or three of the Guards whom I
had come to know through Lescaut to undertake the capture of
G . . . M . . . I found only one in their lodging, but he was an ad-
venturous soul who had no sooner heard what was on foot than he
assured me of its success: he asked only ten pistoles to pay three
soldiers in the Guards whom he meant to employ with himself at
their head. I begged him to lose no time. He had them together in
less than a quarter of an hour, I waited for him at his house, and on
his return with his associates, I guided him myself to the corner of
a street through which G . . . M . . . must pass on his way back to
Manon. I warned him not to mishandle him, but to guard him so
close until seven next morning that I could rest assured of his not
escaping. He told me that he designed to take him to his own
room, make him undress or even put him in his own bed, whilst he
himself would spend the night in drinking and dicing with his
three bravos. I stayed with them up till the moment that I caught
sight of G . . . M . . ., and then withdrew a few steps into a shadowy
corner, that I might be witness of a scene so extraordinary. The
Guardsman accosted him, pistol in hand, and explained to him

courteously that he had no designs either on his money or his life, but that if he made the least difficulty about following him, or uttered the least shout, he would blow his brains out. G . . . M . . ., seeing that he had three soldiers at his back and not anxious for the contents of the pistol, made no resistance. I watched him led away like a sheep. I at once returned to Manon, and to keep the servants from being in any way suspicious, I said to her as I came in that she must not expect M. de G . . . M . . . for supper, that business had cropped up which detained him in spite of himself, and that he had begged me to bear her his excuses and to sup with her, which I should regard as a great favour from so lovely a Lady. She seconded my design, very adroitly. We sat down to table. So long as the lackeys were in the room to wait upon us, we assumed complete gravity, but once they were dismissed, we passed one of the most charming evenings of our lives. I had secretly bidden Marcel to find a cab and bespeak it to be at the door on the morrow before six in the morning. I pretended to leave Manon towards midnight: but, returning by stealth, thanks to Marcel, I made ready to occupy G . . . M . . .'s bed, even as I had filled his place at table. During all this time our evil genius was toiling to destroy us. We were drunk with pleasure, and the sword hung over our heads. The thread that supported it was about to break. But that you may better understand the circumstances of our ruin, I must enlighten you as to the cause.

G . . . M . . . had had a lackey following him at the moment of his arrest by the Guardsman. Terrified at what had befallen his master the fellow turned to flee the way he had come, and the first step that he took to succour him was to go and warn old G . . . M . . . of what had just taken place. Tidings so disquieting could not fail to rouse a good deal of alarm. G . . . M . . . had but this one son, spirited far beyond his years. He would have the lackey tell him everything his son had done that afternoon: if he had fallen out with anyone: if he had taken part in someone else's quarrel: if he had been in some house of ill-fame. The man, believing his master to be in danger of his life and feeling that he must not beat about the bush if he were to save him, revealed all that he knew of his love for Manon, the money he had been out, the fashion in which he had spent the afternoon with her until nine o'clock at night, his leaving the house, and the mishap on his return. It was enough to make the old man suspect that the root of the trouble was a rival's jealousy. Although it was at least half-past ten at night, he did not hesitate to go straight to the Lieutenant of Police. He begged him to give particular instructions to the various Patrols of the Watch; and asking for one of them as his own escort, himself hurried to the street where his son had been arrested; he visited all the places in the town where he might hope to find him, and failing to discover any trace of him, he finally had his escort accompany him to the house of his son's mistress, imagining that the young man might have returned. I was about to get into bed when he arrived. The door of the chamber was closed, so that I had heard no knocking at the street door; but he made his entry followed by two Archers, and after vainly enquiring what had become of his son, he conceived the wish to see his mistress and find if she could throw any light upon it. He came upstairs to the room, still accompanied by his Archers; we were ready to get into bed, the door opened, and the sight of him froze our blood. My God! said I to Manon, it is old G...M...I sprang to my sword. Unluckily, it was entangled in my belt. The Archers, seeing my movement, at once came forward and laid hold on me. A man in his shirt is helpless. They took from me every means I had of defending myself. G...M..., bewildered as he was, was not slow to recognise me. It was still easier for him to recognise Manon. Is it an illusion? said he gravely, do I not see the Chevalier des Grieux and Manon Lescaut? So furious was I with shame and anguish, that I made no answer. For a while he

"The Archers came forward and laid hold on me. A man in his shirt is helpless. They took from me every means of defending myself"

stood, seeming to revolve divers thoughts in his mind, and then, as if they had all at once inflamed his wrath, Wretch! he cried, addressing himself to me, you have killed my son. The insult stung me to the quick. You old villain! I haughtily replied, if I had been minded to kill any of your family, I should have begun with you. Hold him fast, said he to the Archers, he must give me news of my son; if he does not this moment tell me what he has done with him, I shall have him hanged to-morrow. You will have me hanged? I returned. Blackguard! it is the like of you that one looks for on the gallows; know that I am of better and nobler blood than you. Yes, I added, I do know what has happened to your son: and if you anger me further, I shall have him strangled before morning, and I promise you the same fate next. It was imprudent of me to admit to him that I knew where his son was, but the extremity of my anger made me indiscreet. He at once summoned five or six Archers who were in waiting at the door, and bade them secure every servant in the house. Ah, Sir Knight, he went on, mocking, you know where my son is, and you will have him strangled, you say: we shall see to that, be sure. I felt at once what a blunder I had made. He came up to Manon, who was seated crying on the bed; and paid her a few sardonic compliments on the empire she had over father and son, and the good use she made of it. The old Monster of incontinence would even have taken some liberties with her. Beware of touching her! I shouted at him. There is nothing sacred enough to save you from my hands. He went out, leaving three Archers in the room, with instructions to see that we at once put on our clothes.

I do not know what his designs upon us at that moment may have been. Perhaps we might have obtained our liberty by telling him where his son was. I wondered, as I dressed, if that were not the best course open to me; but if such were his mood on leaving the room, it was far other when he returned. He had gone to question Manon's servants, whom the Archers had in custody. He could learn nothing from those that his son had engaged for her: but when he learned that Marcel had hitherto been in our service, he determined to make him speak, intimidating him by threats. The poor fellow was a faithful soul, but simple and ignorant. The memory of what he had done at the Hôpital for Manon's rescue, added to the terror with which G . . . M . . . inspired him, made such an impression on his credulous brain that he thought he was about to be taken to the gallows or the wheel. He promised to reveal everything that had come to his knowledge, if his life would be spared. G . . . M . . . was now convinced that there was something more serious and more criminal about our affair than he had hitherto had reason to suspect. He offered Marcel not only his life, but a reward in return for his confession. The poor soul informed him of part of our design, which we had not hesitated to talk over freely in his presence, as he was to have taken some share in it. True, he was wholly ignorant of the changes made in it since we had come to Paris; but he had been instructed, on leaving Chaillot, in the general plan of the enterprise, and the rôle which he was to play. He confessed to him therefore that we had meant to make a dupe of his son, and that Manon was to receive, or had already received, ten thousand francs, which, according to our way of it, would never return to the heirs of the house of G . . . M . . .

Upon this disclosure, the old man came abruptly upstairs and into our room. Without a word, he passed through to the cabinet, where he had no difficulty in finding the money and the jewels. He came back to us, his countenance inflamed, and holding before us what he was pleased to call our pilfering, overwhelmed us with insults and reproaches. He dangled before Manon the pearl necklace and the bracelets. You recognise them? he asked, with a mocking smile; it is not the first time that you have seen them. The very same, upon my honour! They were to your taste, my beauty, I can well believe that. The poor babes! he added: pretty enough, the

pair of them, i' faith: but a little of the rogue about them, too. My
heart burst with rage at this insulting speech. To be free for one
moment I would have given . . . Just Heaven, what would I not
have given! At last, I did violence to myself so far as to say with a
moderation that was only a refinement of fury: Enough, sir, of this
insolent jesting. What is in hand? Come, what do you intend to do
with us? What is in hand, my young sir, he replied, is quick march
to the Châtelet. To-morrow will bring daylight: we shall have more
light on our affairs, and I hope that you will have the goodness, in
the end, to inform me where my son is. It took little reflection to
make me realise how terrible would be the consequences, let us
once be imprisoned in the Châtelet. I trembled as I foresaw all its
perils. In spite of all my pride, I recognised that I must bend beneath the weight of my destiny, and flatter my most bitter enemy,
to win something from him by submission. I asked him, courteously, to give me a moment's hearing. I condemn myself, Monsieur,
said I, I confess that youth has made me commit grievous faults,
faults from which you have so suffered as to have a right to complain: but if you know the power of love, if you can judge the
suffering of an unhappy young man from whom all that he loves
has been reft, you will perhaps find excuses for my having sought a
trifling vengeance, or at least think me sufficiently punished by the
humiliation I have but now endured. There needs neither prison
nor torture to make me reveal to you where your son is. He is safe;
it was no part of my intention to injure him or to outrage you; I am
ready to give you the name of the place where he is passing a peaceful night, if you will be good enough to give us our freedom. Far
from being touched by my appeal, the old Tiger turned his back
upon us with a laugh. He let fall a few words, sufficient to show me
that he knew our design from its beginning. As far as his son was
concerned, he added harshly, he would soon find his own way
home, since I had not assassinated him. Take them to the Petit-

Châtelet, said he to the Archers: and take care that the Chevalier does not slip through your fingers: the knave has escaped once already from Saint-Lazare.

He went out and left me in a state you may well imagine. O Heaven, I cried, I shall receive with submission whatever blows may come from Thy hand, but that a false rogue should have power to lord it over me thus, this is the last despair. The Archers asked us not to keep them waiting any longer. They had a coach ready at the door. I held out my hand to Manon, to go down. Come, my beloved Queen, said I, come, submit to all the rigour of our fate. Some day, it will perhaps please Heaven to see us happier. We left in the same coach. She put herself in my arms. I had not heard her once open her mouth, since the first moment of G . . . M . . .'s arrival: but, once alone with me, she murmured a thousand endearments, reproaching herself for being the cause of my misfortune. I assured her that I should never complain of my lot so long as she would continue loving me. It is not I who am to be pitied, said I: a few months of prison have no terrors for me, and I should always prefer the Châtelet to Saint-Lazare. But it is for you, dear heart, that my heart is stirred. What a fate for a creature so charming! Heaven! how canst thou treat so harshly the loveliest of thy works? Why were we not born, you and I, with qualities that matched with our misery? We have been given intelligence, taste, sensibility; alas, a sorry use we make of them, whilst so many grovelling souls, worthy of our fate, enjoy all the favours of fortune! Such thoughts as these pierced my heart with grief. But it was as nothing in comparison with the agony of thinking of the future: fear for Manon shrivelled my soul. She had already been in the Hôpital, and even had she left it with full consent, I knew that relapses of this sort were visited with dire penalties. I would fain have told her of my dread; I feared it might be too much for her. I trembled for her, without daring to warn her of the danger, and I clasped her, sighing, in my arms, to assure her at least of my love; it was almost the only feeling I dared utter. Manon, said I, tell me frankly, will you always love me? She made answer that she was very unhappy that I could have any doubt of it. Then, said I, I doubt no longer, and I can outface every enemy we have with that assurance. I shall avail myself of my family to get out of the Châtelet, and every drop of my blood will be good for nothing, if I do not snatch you from it as soon as I myself am free. We arrived at the prison. They put us in different quarters. I had foreseen it, or it would have been a cruel blow. I recommended Manon to the care of the Concierge, telling him that I was a man of some note, and promising him a generous recompense. I embraced my poor mistress before leaving her. I implored her not to grieve overmuch, and to fear nothing as long as I was on the earth. I was not without money. Some of it I gave to her, and out of what I kept I paid the Concierge for a month's full board in advance, for herself and me.

My money had a very good effect. They put me in a neatly furnished room, and assured me that Manon had the like. At once I set my wits to work on plans for my speedy liberation. It was clear that there was nothing absolutely criminal in this affair: and though the intention of theft might be proved by Marcel's confession, I knew very well that one is not punished for merely willing a crime. I resolved to write at once to my father, and beg him to come in person to Paris. I was much less ashamed, as I have already said, of being in the Châtelet than of being in Saint-Lazare. Besides, although I retained all the respect due to a father's authority, age and experience had greatly lessened my timidity. I wrote my letter, and they made no difficulty at the Châtelet about letting it be sent, but it was a trouble I might have spared myself, if I had known that my father was to arrive in Paris on the morrow. He had received the letter I had written him a week earlier. It had given him the liveliest pleasure: but however flattering the hopes I had held out of my conversion, he had judged it wiser not to rely wholly on my promises. He had made the decision to come and satisfy himself of my reformation with his own eyes, and to determine his own conduct by the sincerity of my repentance. He arrived on the day following my imprisonment. His first visit was paid to Tiberge, to whom I had begged him to address his reply. He could not learn from him either my address or my present condition, but only my outstanding adventures, since my escape from Saint-Sulpice. Tiberge gave him a very favourable account of the inclinations towards goodness which I had shown in my last interview with him. He added that he thought I had severed myself completely from Manon: but that he was nevertheless surprised at having heard nothing of me for a week. My father was no fool. He felt that there was something in the silence Tiberge complained of that had escaped his penetration, and set himself so busily to tracing me that within two days of his arrival he learned that I was in the Châtelet. Before receiving his visit, which I was far from expecting so soon, I had one from the Lieutenant-General of Police; or rather, to call things by their right names, I underwent examination. He made me a few reproaches, but they were neither harsh nor discourteous. He told me gently enough that he grieved at my ill conduct: that I had been very foolish to make an enemy such as M. de G . . . M . . .: that it was indeed easy to see that there was more recklessness and levity in my offence than malice: nevertheless, it was the second time that I had come before his tribunal, and he had hoped I might have become wiser after my two or three months' lessoning at Saint-Lazare. Delighted at having to do with so reasonable a judge, I made him my explanations in a fashion so respectful and so restrained that he seemed thoroughly satisfied with my replies. He told me that I must not fret overmuch, and that he was inclined to do what he could for me, in consideration of my birth and my youth. I ventured to speak to him for Manon, and urged her sweetness and the goodness of her nature. He made answer with a laugh that he had not yet seen her, but that she had been described to him as a very dangerous character. That word so roused my tenderness that I said a thousand passionate things in defence of my poor mistress: and could not even keep myself from shedding a few tears. He gave orders to have me taken back to my room. Love! Love! exclaimed the sober Magistrate as he watched me go, will you and wisdom never be reconciled?

I was sorrowfully busy with my thoughts, and going over in my mind the conversation I had had with the Lieutenant-General, when I heard my door open; it was my father. Although I ought to have been half prepared for it, expecting him as I did within the next few days, the sight of him so shook me that if the earth had opened at my feet, I should gladly have flung myself into its depths. I went forward to embrace him, in the utmost embarrassment. He sat down; neither of us had opened our lips. As I still remained standing, with downcast eyes and uncovered head, Sit down, sir, said he gravely, sit down. Thanks to the open scandal of your debauchery and knaveries, I was able to trace your whereabouts. It is the advantage of merit such as yours, it cannot long be hid. You go to fame by an infallible road. Its goal, I trust, will shortly be La Grève, and you will actually have the glory of being exhibited there to the admiration of us all. I made no answer. Unhappy, he went on, is that father, who has tenderly loved a son, spared no pains to make an honourable man of him, and finds at last nothing but a rascal to disgrace him! One can find comfort after a blow of Fortune: time can efface it, the vexation dies: but where is the remedy for an evil that goes still increasing, the disorders of a vicious son, lost to all sense of honour? Not a word to say, wretch? he added. There's modesty well dissembled, a sweet hypocrite, faith: would not one take him for the most honourable gentleman of his house?

Although I had to recognise that I deserved some part of these insults, yet it seemed to me that they were carried too far. I thought it might be permitted simply to explain what was in my mind. I assure you, Sir, said I, that the confusion you see in me is in no way feigned: it is the natural state of a son, not ill conditioned, before a father whom he holds in infinite respect, above all a father incensed. I make no pretence to be the most orderly member of our race. I know that I deserve your reproaches, but I do implore you to put a little more kindness into them, and not to treat me as if I were the most infamous of men. I do not deserve names so harsh as these. It is love, and you know it, that has caused all my faults. Oh mortal passion! Alas, do you yourself not know its strength, and can it be that your blood, from which my own blood springs, has never pulsed with the same ardours? Love has made me too tender, too passionate, too faithful, perhaps too indulgent to the desires of a mistress who is all charm: these are my crimes. Is there one among them that disgraces you? Come, my dear father, I added affectionately, some pity for a son who has always respected you, always loved you; who has not, as you think, renounced honour and duty, and who is a thousand times more to be pitied than you could conceive. As I finished speaking I let fall some tears.

A father's heart is the masterpiece of Nature; there, so to speak, she reigns indulgent and rules its every spring. My father, who was in addition a man of wit and taste, was so moved by the turn I had given my defence that he could not master himself to hide the change in him. Come here, my poor Chevalier, said he, come and kiss me: you make me sorry for you. I kissed him. He held me to him in such fashion that I could judge what was passing in his heart. Come now, he went on, what are we to do to get you out of this? Tell me the whole story, without any disguising. As there was nothing, after all, in the bulk of my conduct to my absolute disgrace, at any rate in comparison with the young men of a certain condition, and since the keeping of a mistress does not brand one with infamy in these days, any more than a little skill in attracting the luck of the gaming-table, I gave my father a candid account of the life I had led. To every fault which I confessed I took care to add illustrious examples, to diminish the shame of it. I lived with a mistress, said I, without the bonds of the marriage ceremony: M. le duc de ... keeps two, in the sight of all Paris; M. de F ... has had one for the last ten years, and loves her with a fidelity he has never given his wife. Two-thirds of Parisian society preen themselves on it. I have used some sleight of hand at cards: M. le Marquis de ... and the Count de ... have no other source of income: the Prince de ... and M. le Duc de ... are the leaders of a band of Knights of the same Order. As for my designs on the purse of the two G ... M ..., I could have proved easily enough that I did not lack precedents: but I had too much sense of honour left not to condemn myself equally with those whose examples I might have cited: and so I did but beg my father to condone my fault by the violence of the two passions which had shaken me: revenge and love. He asked me if I could give him any suggestion as to the readiest means of obtaining my liberty, above all in such a way as to avoid open scandal. I told him of the kindliness with which the Lieutenant-General of Police regarded me. If you find any difficulties, I said, it will be from the G ... M ... quarter, and so I think it well if you could bring yourself to go and see them. He promised me that he would. I did not dare ask him to intercede for Manon. It was not from any lack of hardihood, but from the fear I was in of outraging him by such a proposal, and so provoking him to some design that would be fatal to herself and me. I do not know to this day if this fear were not the cause of my worst misfortunes, in that it kept me from sounding my father's mood, and making efforts to bring him to a frame of mind more favourable to my poor mistress. I might perhaps once more have stirred his pity. I might have put him on his guard against the impressions which he was to receive too readily from old G . . . M . . . How can I tell? My evil star might have triumphed over all my efforts: but at least I should have only that, and my enemies' cruelty, to blame for my unhappiness.

After leaving me, my father went to pay a visit to M. de G . . . M . . . He found him with his son, whom my Guardsman had punctiliously set at liberty. I have never learned the particulars of their conversation: but it has been only too easy for me to judge of it from its fatal results. They went together, the two fathers, that is, to the Lieutenant-General of Police, and asked of him two favours; the one, to let me at once leave the Châtelet; the other, to imprison Manon for the rest of her days, or to send her to America. About that time they were beginning to ship a good many vagrants to the Mississippi. The Lieutenant-General of Police gave them his word that Manon should be sent off by the first boat. M. de G . . . M . . . and my father came together to bring me the news of my liberty. M. de G . . . M . . . made some civil reference to the past, and congratulating me on my good fortune in having such a father, exhorted me to profit henceforward by his instruction and example. My father bade me make him my apologies for the attempted injury I had offered his family, and thank him for having busied himself together with him towards my liberation. We came out together, with not a word said of my mistress. I dared not even speak of her to the Gatekeepers in their presence. Alas! my sorry recommendations would have been useless enough! The cruel order had come at the same time as that for my enlargement. The unhappy girl was taken an hour later to the Hôpital, there to join certain other unfortunates condemned to the same fate. As my father had obliged me to follow him to the house where he was staying, it was almost six o'clock in the evening before I found a chance to slip out of his sight and go back to the Châtelet. I had no plan beyond conveying some comforts to Manon and commending her to the Concierge, for I had no hope that I would be granted permission to see her. I had not yet had time to think out plans for her rescue.

I asked to speak to the Concierge. He had been well pleased with my generosity and gentleness, and feeling kindly towards me as he did, he spoke to me of Manon's fate as a misfortune which he was heartily sorry for, since it would distress me. I did not grasp his meaning. We talked for a few moments without understanding each other. At last, seeing that I stood in need of enlightenment, he gave me that which it has already been my dreadful task to tell you, and must be again to repeat. Never did a seizure of apoplexy have a swifter and more terrible effect. I fell, with so agonising a throbbing at my heart that even as I lost consciousness I thought myself set free from life for ever. Something of that thought stayed with me even when I came back to myself: I turned my gaze all round the room and on myself, to make sure that I had still the misery of being a living man. Assuredly, if I had followed only the natural impulse which would fain set one's self free of one's sorrows, nothing, in that moment of despair and consternation, could have seemed to me sweeter than death. Religion itself could make me envisage nothing in the life after death more unendurable than the convulsions which tortured me. Yet, by one of love's own miracles, I soon gathered strength enough to thank Heaven for having restored me to consciousness and reason. My death would have availed me only: Manon had need that I should live to avenge her. I vowed to commit myself thereto without restraint or sparing. The Concierge saw to me as kindly as if he had been the best friend I had. I accepted his services with a lively gratitude. Alas! I said to him, so you are moved by my grief. Everyone abandons me. Even my father is doubtless one of my cruellest persecutors. No one has pity on me. You, in this abode of harshness and savagery, you alone show compassion on the most miserable of men. He advised me not to show myself in the street until I was a little recov-

ered from the agitation I was in. Let be, let be, said I as I went out, I shall see you sooner than you think. Get ready the blackest of your cells for me: I have work to do that will deserve it. In very truth, my first resolves stopped nothing short of doing away with the two, G . . . M . . . and the Lieutenant-General of Police, and then of armed assault upon the Hôpital with every soul I could enlist in my quarrel. My father himself would hardly have been respected in a vengeance which seemed to me so just; for the concierge had not hidden from me that he and G . . . M . . . were the authors of my ruin. But when I had walked a pace or two in the streets, and the air had something refreshed my heat and disorder, fury gave place little by little to more reasonable considerations. The death of our enemies would do poor service to Manon, and would doubtless expose me to see every means of aiding her taken from me. Besides, could I have recourse to cowardly assassination? What other course was open to my vengeance? I collected all my strength and all my wits and set them to work on Manon's rescue, postponing all the rest till after the success of that main enterprise. I had little money left. That, nevertheless, was the essential foundation, which must first be laid. I could see only three persons from whom I could hope: M. de T . . ., my father, and Tiberge. There was little likelihood of getting anything from the last two, and I was ashamed to weary the other with my importunities. But despair has few scruples. I went straight to the Seminary at Saint-Sulpice, without concerning myself as to possible recognition: I had Tiberge sent for. His first words showed me that he as yet knew nothing of my most recent adventures. This changed the plan I had formed of softening him by compassion. I spoke to him vaguely of the pleasure I had had in again seeing my father, and begged him frankly to lend me some money, pretending that before I left Paris I wanted to pay a few debts which I preferred to say nothing about. He at once gave me his purse. I took five hundred *livres* from the six that I found in it.

I offered him my note of hand; he was too generous to accept it.

From thence I went to the house of M. de T . . . I kept nothing from him. I told him the story of my misfortunes and my griefs; he was already acquaint with it to the smallest detail, thanks to the pains he had been at to follow the adventures of young G . . . M . . . None the less he listened to me, and gave me his sympathy. When I asked him for advice on how to rescue Manon, he sadly made answer that he saw so little prospect of it, that short of a miracle from heaven, one might give up hope: that he had gone straight to the Hôpital as soon as she was imprisoned there: that he had not been able to obtain even for himself permission to see her: that the orders of the Lieutenant-General of Police were of the utmost strictness, and, for crowning misfortune, the unhappy company which she was to join were destined to set out the day after to-morrow. Such was my consternation as I listened that he might have gone on speaking for an hour before I should have thought of interrupting him. He went on to say that he had expressly not gone to see me at the Châtelet that he might not be suspected of any understanding with me, and so might have more opportunity of doing me service: during the hours that had passed since my leaving it he had been ill at ease to know where I had betaken myself, and that he had wished to see me at once, to suggest to me the only measure from which he could see any hope of an alteration in Manon's fate: a dangerous measure, in which he begged me to keep eternal silence as to his share: it was to find a few bravos, hardy enough to attack Manon's Escort once they had left Paris with her. He did not wait for me to tell him of my poverty: Here, said he, giving me a purse, here are a hundred pistoles that may be of some use to you. You can pay them back to me when fortune has put your affairs to rights again. He added that if his reputation had allowed him to attempt in his own person the rescue of my mistress, he would have offered me his arm and sword.

This extraordinary generosity moved me to tears. To show him my gratitude, I spent whatever ardour my suffering had left me. I asked him if there was nothing to hope from intercession with the Lieutenant-General of Police. He told me that he had thought of it, but judged it a poor resource, since a favour of that kind cannot be asked for without a motive, and he did not see what motive one could use to secure the sympathy of a man of influence and weight: whatever one could hope to do in that quarter, could only be by bringing about a change of heart in M. de G . . . and my father, and pledging them to ask themselves a revocation of his sentence from the Lieutenant-General of Police. He offered to do all he could to win over the younger G . . . M . . ., although he thought him a little cooled towards him, thanks to some suspicions of his part in our affair, and he urged me to leave nothing undone, on my side, to bend my father's temper.

It was no light undertaking; I say this not only from the natural difficulty I should have in winning him over, but for another reason which made me dread even going near him: I had stolen out of his lodging against his orders, and I was fully determined not to go back there, once I learned the sorrowful fate which awaited Manon. I feared with good reason that he might keep me in custody in spite of myself, and might even take me back with him to the Country. My elder brother had already taken that way of it. It is true that I was older now: but years are a poor argument against force. However, I thought of a plan which would save me from that risk: it was to send for him to some public spot, and announce myself to him under another name. I took at once that course. M. de T . . . set off to see G . . . M . . ., and I to the Luxembourg, whence I sent word to my father that a Gentleman of his following was awaiting him. I feared that he might find some difficulty in coming, for it was already beginning to grow dark. Nevertheless he appeared shortly, followed by his man. I begged him to choose an alley where we

could be alone. We walked a hundred paces at least, without a
word spoken. He could easily conjecture, no doubt, that so many
preparations had not been made for nothing. He waited for my
appeal, and I reflected on the framing of it. At last I found my
tongue. Sir, said I, trembling, you are a kind father, you have overwhelmed me with favours, and you have forgiven an infinity of
faults. Heaven is my witness that I have towards you all the sentiments of the most devoted and most respectful son. But it seems to
me ... that your sternness ... Well? My sternness? interrupted my
father, to whom I doubtless seemed to speak too slowly for his
impatience. Ah Sir, I went on, it seems to me that your sternness is
extreme in the treatment you have meted out to the unhappy
Manon. You referred yourself to M. de G ... M ... His hatred pictured her to you in the blackest colours. You have formed a horrible
idea of her. Yet she is the sweetest, the most lovable creature that
ever lived. Had it but pleased Heaven to put it in your heart to see
her for one moment, I am no surer that she is charming than I am
that you would have found her so. You would have taken her part.
You would have loathed the black plots of G ... M ... You would
have had pity on her and on me. Alas! I am sure of it. Your heart is
not insensible, you would have let yourself be softened. Again he
interrupted me, seeing that I spoke with a heat that would not
readily suffer me to make an end. He wished to know what I was
aiming at by making such a passionate speech. I am asking you for
my life, I made answer, which I cannot keep for a moment, once
Manon sets out for America. No, no, said he sternly, I would rather
see you without life, than without decency and honour. Then let us
go no further, I cried, stopping him by the arm, take it from me,
this hateful, intolerable life: for in the despair you have flung me
into, death will be a grace; it is a gift worthy a father's hand. I
should be giving you no more than you deserve, he retorted. I
know plenty of fathers who would not have waited so long to be

themselves your executioners: but it is my own too great indulgence that has ruined you. I flung myself at his feet. Ah, if aught of
it is left, I cried, clasping his knees, do not harden yourself against
my tears. Think that I am your son . . . Alas! bethink yourself of
my mother. You loved her so tenderly. Would you have suffered
her to be torn from your arms? You would have defended her till
death. Have not others a heart too? Can one be cruel after once
having known what tenderness and grief can be? No more of your
mother, he returned, anger in his tone, the memory of her kindles
my indignation. Your debauchery would have killed her with grief,
had she lived to see it. Enough of this, he added, it only annoys me,
and will never make me change my mind. I am going back to my
house. I command you to follow me. The harsh and dry tone of the
command showed me too plainly that his heart was immovable. I
took a few paces away from him, fearing lest he should try to seize
me with his own hands. Do not add to my despair, said I, by
forcing me to disobey you. It is impossible for me to follow you. It
is no less so for me to live, after the harshness with which you are
treating me. Therefore, I bid you an eternal farewell. My death,
which you will soon learn, I added sadly, will perhaps bring my
father's heart to me again. I turned to leave him. So you refuse to
follow me, he cried, in a heat of anger. Go, rush on your ruin. Farewell, graceless and rebellious son! Farewell, said I in my frenzy,
farewell, barbarous and unnatural father!

I came out at once from the Luxembourg. I walked the streets
like a madman, as far as M. de T . . .'s house. As I walked, I lifted
my eyes and my hands to invoke all the powers of Heaven. O
Heaven! said I, wilt thou be as pitiless as men? I have no help to
look for save from thee. M. de T . . . was not yet returned but he
came back after I had been waiting for him a few moments. His
negotiations had succeeded no better than my own. He told me so,
with downcast looks. The younger G . . . M . . . though less in-

censed than his father against Manon and myself, had no wish to undertake to intercede with him on our behalf. He had shielded himself by instancing the fear he himself was in of the vindictive old man, who was already in high displeasure against him, reproaching him with his intended intercourse with Manon. The only course now left me was that of violence, such as M. de T . . . had outlined to me: to it were all my hopes reduced. They are uncertain enough, said I, but the surest comfort for me is that at least I shall die in the attempt. I left him, begging him to aid me by his prayers, and my sole thought now was to assemble round me comrades to whom I could impart some spark of my courage and my resolution.

The first man to occur to me was the same Guardsman whom I had employed in the arrest of G . . . M . . . I had planned moreover to go and spend the night in his room, for I had been too much preoccupied during the afternoon to provide myself with a lodging. I found him alone. He was delighted to see me safe out of the Châtelet, and affectionately offered me his services. I explained what it was I wished of him. He had sense enough to see all the difficulties, but generosity enough to undertake to surmount them. We spent part of the night in working out my plan. He spoke of the three soldiers in the Guards whom he had employed in the last affair, as stout fellows in a pinch. M. de T . . . had given me the exact number of the Archers who were to escort Manon: there were only six. Five hardy and determined men would suffice to strike terror into those poltroons, who are not capable of putting up an honest defence, if cowardice will serve their turn; as I had no lack of money, the Guardsman advised me to spare nothing to assure the success of our attack. We must have horses, said he, and pistols, and a musket each. I'll make it my business to-morrow to see to the preparations. And we must have civilian dress for our three soldiers, for they dare not appear in an affair of this sort in the uniform of the Regiment. I handed over to him the hundred pistoles which M.

de T . . . had given me. They were spent next day to the last half-penny. The three soldiers were paraded before me. I fired them with great promises, and to cure them of any misgiving, I began with a present to each one of them of ten pistoles. The appointed day came. I sent one of them very early to the Hôpital, to make sure with his own eyes of the moment that the Archers would set off with their prey. Although I only took this precaution in a fit of uneasiness and foreboding, it turned out to be absolutely necessary. I had relied on false information which had been given me as to the route, and being convinced that it was at La Rochelle this unhappy band were to be embarked, I should have waited for them on the road to Orleans, and lost my pains. Now I was informed, thanks to my soldier's report, that they would take the road to Normandy, and that it was from Havre-de-Grâce they would set out for America. We straightway made our way to the Porte Saint-Honoré, taking care to go by different streets. We assembled again outside the Faubourg; our horses were fresh. It was not long before we descried the six guards and the two wretched waggons that you saw at Passy two years ago. The sight all but took my strength and consciousness from me. O Fortune! I cried, cruel Fortune, grant me here, at least, death or victory. We held council for a moment as to the plan of our attack. The Archers were hardly more than four hundred yards in front, and we could intercept them by crossing a little field round which the high road wound. The Guardsman was inclined to that course, so as to burst on them all at once, and take them by surprise. I agreed with him, and I was the first to put spurs to my horse; but fortune had pitilessly rejected my vows. The Archers, seeing five Horsemen riding down upon them, never doubted but that they were to be attacked. They put themselves on the defensive, fixing their bayonets and levelling their muskets resolutely enough. That sight, which did but rouse the Guardsman and myself, took every scrap of courage from our poltroon companions. They pulled up as if by consent, and after a word or two among themselves which I did not hear, turned their horses' heads, and were off hell for leather on the Paris road. My God! said the Guardsman, who seemed as aghast as myself at this infamous desertion, what are we to do, there are only two of us now. I had lost my voice, in astonishment and anger. I pulled up, uncertain whether my first vengeance should not be to pursue and chastise the scoundrels who had left me. I watched them flee one way, and again turned my eyes upon the Archers. If I could have been in two places at once, I should have hurled myself at the same moment upon both objects of my wrath. I glowered upon them both. The Guardsman, guessing my uncertainty from the wildness of my eyes, implored me to listen to his advice. Now that we are but two, he said, it would be madness to attack six men as well armed as ourselves, and evidently ready to put up a good fight. Better go back to Paris, and try for better luck in choosing our men. The Archers cannot make long stages with two heavy coaches: we shall overtake them to-morrow easily. I gave a moment's reflection to his proposal: but, seeing on all sides nothing but despair, I took a truly desperate resolve: it was to thank my companion for his services, and, far from attacking the Archers, to go and ask them humbly if I might join their troop, so as to accompany Manon as far as Havre-de-Grâce, and then go overseas with her. The whole world is turned persecutor or traitor, said I to my Guardsman, I have no more trust in any. I count no more on fortune nor on the help of men. My illhap is at its height: nothing is left me now but to submit. And so I close my eyes against all hope. May Heaven reward your generosity. Farewell, I go to aid my destiny in achieving my ruin, for I rush upon it of my own free will. In vain he tried to persuade me to come back to Paris. I begged him to leave me to follow my resolve, and to quit me on the spot, lest the Archers should continue to think that we meant to attack.

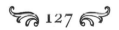

I made my way towards them, at so slow a pace and with a countenance so disheartened that they could have found nothing to fear in my approach. None the less, they still stood on the defensive. Set your minds at rest, gentlemen, said I, as I came up, I wage no war with you: I do but come to ask a favour from you. I begged them to take the road without suspicion, and on the way I told them the favours I hoped to have from them. They consulted together as to how they should receive this overture. The Leader of the company was spokesman for the rest. His answer was that they had the strictest orders to watch their prisoners: but that I seemed such a pretty fellow, he and his mates would relax a little of their duty: but that I must understand it would cost me something. I had still about fifteen pistoles left: I told them frankly all that was in my purse. Well, well, said the Archer, we'll be generous with you. It will only cost you a crown an hour to chat with whichever of our wenches takes your fancy most; 'tis the regular price at Paris. I had not made particular mention of Manon, for I was not minded that they should come to know my passion. At first they took it that it was only a young man's whim to amuse himself a while with these poor souls: but once they thought to detect the lover in me, they so raised the tariff that my purse was exhausted on our leaving Mantes, where we had lain the night before we arrived at Passy.

Must I tell you what was the sorrowful subject of my talks with Manon during that journey, or the first impression of the sight of her when I had got leave from the Guards to draw near her waggon! Ah, words can never but half express the feelings of the heart; but imagine for yourself my poor Mistress chained by the waist, seated on some handfuls of straw, her head leant despairingly against the side of the waggon, her face white and wet with streaming tears that forced their way beneath the eyelids that she kept perpetually closed. She had not even had the curiosity to open them when she heard the commotion among the Guards at the moment of our threatened attack. Her linen was soiled and disordered; her delicate hands bare to the harshness of the air: all that enchanting frame, the face that could bring back the universe to idolatry, was sunk in unutterable abandonment and despair. I spent some time watching her, riding alongside the waggon. I was so little myself, that I was more than once on the verge of a dangerous fall. My sighs, my occasional interjections, roused her to glance towards me. She recognised me, and I saw that at the first impulse, she tried to throw herself out of the waggon to come to me: but, held back by her chain, relapsed into her original attitude. I implored the Archers to stop a moment for pity's sake: for greed's sake they consented. I got down from my horse so as to sit beside her. She was so languid and so exhausted that it was a long time before she could speak, or lift her hands. Meantime they were drenched with my tears; myself unable to speak a single word, we sat there, as sorrowfully placed a pair as the world has known. Our words, when at last we were able to speak, were no less sorrowful. Manon spoke little: shame and grief seemed to have affected the chords of her voice; its tone was faint and tremulous. She thanked me for not having forgotten her, and for giving her the satisfaction, she said it sighing, of seeing me once more, and bidding me a last goodbye. But when I assured her that nothing could separate me from her, and that I was bent on following her to the ends of the earth, to take care of her, to serve her, to love her, to bind for ever my ill-starred destiny to hers, the poor girl's abandonment was so tender, so agonising, that I feared for her very life. Every emotion of her soul seemed centred in her eyes. She kept them fixed upon me. Sometimes she opened her lips, but had not strength to finish the few words she tried to speak. Yet some escaped her: broken phrases of wonder at my love, tender chiding of its excess, doubts that she could be so happy as to have roused in me so absolute a passion, pleading to make me give up the idea of following her, and to seek elsewhere a happiness

worthy of me, which she said I could not hope to find with her.

Despite the most cruel of all fates, I found my blessedness in her gaze, and in the certainty I had of her loving me. I had lost indeed all that other men value; but I was master of the heart of Manon, the only good I cared for. To live in Europe, to live in America, what cared I where I lived, since I was sure of happiness, if I but lived with Manon. Is not the entire universe the native country of two faithful lovers? Father, mother, kinsfolk, friends, riches and happiness, do they not find these in one another? If anything caused me uneasiness, it was my fear of seeing Manon exposed to want. I imagined myself already with her in a barren land, inhabited by Savages. I am very sure, I said, that there could be none so cruel as G...M... and my father. At least they will let us live in peace. If the tales one hears of them are true, they follow the laws of nature. They are ignorant alike of the frenzy of avarice which possesses G...M..., and the fantastic ideas of honour which have made my father my enemy. They will not trouble two lovers whom they see living as innocently as they do. And so on that score I was at peace. But I had no Romantic notions upon the ordinary necessities of life. I had proved too often that there are some deprivations that are unendurable, above all for a delicate girl accustomed to an easy and luxurious life. I was in despair at having uselessly exhausted my purse, and that thanks to the knavery of the Archers I was about to be robbed of the little I had left. I believed that with a certain sum I could have hoped not only to keep myself from actual want for some time in America, where money was scarce, but even to enter on some undertaking that might give me a regular livelihood. This consideration brought it into my mind to write to Tiberge, whom I had always found so ready to offer me a friendly hand. I wrote from the first town that we passed through. I instanced no further reason than the pressing need which I foresaw would be mine on reaching Havre-de-Grâce, whither I confessed to him that I was going to escort Manon. I asked him for a hundred pistoles. Have them ready for me at Havre, said I, with the Post Master. You can realise that it is the last time I shall importune your love for me, and now that my unhappy mistress is to be reft from me for ever, I cannot let her go without some few solaces that might alleviate her lot and my own mortal grief.

The Archers became so intractable once they had discovered the violence of my passion, that by continually redoubling the price of their least favours they soon reduced me to the utmost poverty. Love, moreover, would hardly suffer me to spare my purse. From morning to night I forgot all else beside Manon, and time was measured for me no longer by the hour, but by the whole length of days. My purse at last was empty, and now I found myself exposed to the whims and brutality of six rascals, who treated me with insufferable insolence. You were witness of it at Passy. My encounter with you was the one happy moment of reprieve which Fortune suffered me. Your compassion at sight of my grief was my sole recommendation to your generous heart. The help which you so freely bestowed sufficed me to reach Havre, and the Archers kept their promise more faithfully than I had hoped. We arrived at Havre. I went straight to the post-office. Tiberge had not yet had time to reply. I found out the exact day on which I might expect his letter. It could only come two days later, and by a strange dispensation of my evil destiny, it so happened that our ship was to sail on the morning of the day on which I expected the post. I cannot convey to you what was my despair. What! I cried, even in misfortune itself, am I still to be notorious by excess! Alas! said Manon, is a life so unhappy worth the care we take of it? let us die at Havre, my dearest, at one blow make an end of all our misery. Are we to drag it still into an unknown land, where doubtless the last extremes of horror must await us, since I know that there must be a judgment on me. Let us die, she said again, or at least put me to death, and go to find a better fate in the arms of a less hapless love. No, no, said I, 'tis a fate enviable enough for me to be unhappy with you. Her words made me quail. I judged that she was overwhelmed by her misfortunes. I forced myself to appear more tranquil, so as to banish those fatal thoughts of death and of despair. I resolved to abide by that rule in future; and I have proved in consequence that nothing so inspires a woman with courage as the dauntlessness of the man she loves.

Realising that I must hope for no help from Tiberge, I sold my horse. The money from that, added to what was left me of your generosity, amounted to the small sum of seventeen pistoles. I expended seven of these in buying a few necessary comforts for Manon, and carefully locked away the remaining ten, as the foundation of our fortune and our hopes in America. I had no difficulty in being taken on board ship. In those days they cast about on all sides for young folk willing to join the Colony of their own accord. My passage and my keep were offered me gratis. As the Post for Paris was to leave on the morrow, I sent with it a letter for Tiberge. It was touching enough, and must have stirred him to the utmost since it made him take a resolution which could only have risen from an infinite depth of tenderness and generosity towards an unhappy friend.

We set sail. The wind was continually in our favour. I obtained from the Captain a private spot for Manon and myself. He had the goodness to look on us with a kindlier eye than on the bulk of our wretched companions. I had taken him aside on the first day, and, in order to secure some consideration from him, had revealed to him part of my misfortunes. I did not think that I was guilty of a shameful lie in telling him that I was married to Manon. He made as though to believe it: and assured me his protection. We had proof of it throughout the whole voyage. He saw to it that we were properly fed, and the attention which he showed us served to make us respected by our companions in misery. It was my continual preoccupation that no least inconvenience should be allowed to touch Manon. It did not escape her, and that perception, coupled with a lively sense of the strange extremity to which I had reduced myself for her, made her so tender and so passionate, so attentive to my slightest wants, that there sprang up between her and me a perpetual rivalry of service and love. I had no regrets for Europe; on the contrary, the nearer we approached America, the larger and more tranquil felt my heart; if I could have been sure that the absolute necessities of life would not be wanting, I should have thanked Fate for giving so favourable a turn to our misfortunes.

After a voyage of two months, we touched at last on the desired shore. At first sight, the country offered scant attraction. The land stretched barren and uninhabited, here and there a clump of reeds, or a few windstripped trees. No trace of men or animals. However, once the Captain had discharged a few of our guns, we soon perceived a company of the Townsfolk of New Orleans coming toward us with the liveliest tokens of delight. We had not been able to see the town: it is hidden from the sea by a small hill. We were welcomed like people descended from heaven. The poor folk swarmed about us to ask a thousand questions about the state of France and the various Provinces of their birth. They embraced us like brothers, like beloved comrades who had come to share their poverty and their loneliness. We took along with them the road to the town: but we were surprised to find on our approach that what had been vaunted up till then as a fine city was only a gathering of a few poor cabins. There were five or six hundred inhabitants. The Governor's house seemed to us a little distinguished from the rest by its height and its position. It was defended by some earthen outworks, round which ran a broad moat.

We were first presented to him. He had a long talk in private with the Captain, and then, coming back to us, inspected, one after the other, all the girls who had come by that ship. They were thirty in number, for we had found another company at Havre, waiting to join our own. The Governor, after a prolonged examination, summoned various young men of the town, pining in expectation of a bride. The prettiest he gave to the more important, the rest were cast lots for. He had not yet spoken to Manon, but when the others had been ordered to withdraw, he bade us both to stay behind. I learn from the Captain, said he, that you are married, and that he recognised you on the voyage out as two folk of intelligence and desert. I shall not enter into the reasons which brought about your illhap: but if it is true that you have as much breeding as your face is warrant of, I shall spare no pains to mitigate your lot, and you yourselves will play your part in helping me to find some pleasure in this wild and desolate spot. I answered him in the fashion I thought most likely to confirm the impression he had of us. He gave orders for us to be provided with a lodging in the town, and kept us to supper with him. I was surprised to find so much breeding in the head of a company of wretched exiles. He asked us no questions in public on the matter of our adventures. The conversation was general, and in spite of our dejection we forced ourselves, both Manon and myself, to do our share in making it agreeable.

That evening, he had us taken to the dwelling which had been got ready for us. We found a wretched hovel, built of planks and clay, consisting of two rooms on the ground floor, and a loft above. Two or three chairs had been put into it, and a few of the commodities necessary to life. Manon looked aghast at the sight of so forlorn a dwelling, but her distress was for me, far more than for herself. She sat down as soon as we were alone, and began to weep bitterly. I tried at first to comfort her; but when I gathered from her that it was I alone she pitied, and that in our common misfortune she only cared for what I must suffer, I affected courage and even gaiety enough to inspire it in her. What have I to complain of? said I. I possess everything I desire. You love me, do you not? What other happiness have I ever aimed at? Leave the care of our fortunes to Heaven. They do not seem to me so desperate. The Governor is a man of the world: he has shown us consideration: he will not suffer us to lack the necessaries of life. And as for the poverty of our hut and the rudeness of our furniture, you may have noticed that there seem few people here better housed or better furnished than ourselves; and then you are a marvellous Alchemist, I added, kissing her, you transform everything to gold. You will be the richest person in the world, then, she made answer: for if there never was such a love as yours, even so no one could be loved so tenderly as I love you. I am my own judge, she went on. I feel too well that I have never deserved the amazing tenderness you have for me. I have done you injuries that you could not have forgiven me unless out of the utmost goodness. I have been fickle and light, and even loving you madly as I always have, I was wholly graceless. But you could not believe how I have changed. The tears which you have so often seen me shed since we left France have never once been for my own misfortunes. I ceased to feel them as soon as you began to share them. I have only wept out of tenderness and compassion for you. I cannot be comforted for having hurt you for a single moment in my life. I never cease blaming myself for my inconstancy, and my heart melts to see what love has made you do for a wretch who was not worthy of it, and who could not atone even with her blood, she added, in a flood of tears, for half the sorrows she has cost you. Her tears, her words, and the tone in which they were uttered affected me so violently it seemed to me my heart was breaking in twain. Take care, said I, take care, beloved; I have not strength enough to bear such tokens of your love: I am not used to this excess of joy. O God! I cried, I ask no more: I am assured of Manon's heart; and 'tis all I have ever wished to give me happiness: I can never be unhappy now: felicity secure and firm at last. It is, she answered, if you make it depend on me; and I know where to look for mine. I went to rest in that enchantment: my hovel became a Palace worthy of the proudest King. Hereafter, America seemed to me a place of delights. It is to New Orleans that they must come, I would often say to Manon, who would enjoy the true sweetness of love. It is here that one loves without self-interest, without jealousy, without inconstancy. Our fellow countrymen came here to search for gold, they do not conceive that we have found here a far richer treasure.

We were careful to cultivate the friendship of the Governor. He was kind enough, some weeks after our arrival, to give me a minor post which had just fallen vacant at the Fort; although it had no great distinction, I accepted it as a boon from Heaven. It put me in a position to live at no man's charge. I took a man to wait on myself, a maid for Manon. Our little income was arranged. I was orderly in my habits: Manon no less so. We lost no opportunity of doing a service or a kindness to our Neighbours; this obligingness and the gentleness of our bearing won us the trust and affection of the whole colony. In a short time we were so well thought of, that next to the Governor, we ranked as the first people in the town.

The innocence of our pursuits and the unbroken tranquillity in which we lived served to recall us, little by little, to a spirit of devotion and of religion. Manon had never been irreligious, nor had I been one of those extravagant freethinkers who make it their glory to add impiety to the depravity of their morals. Love and youth had caused all our excesses. Experience was beginning to take the place of age: it brought us something of the effect of years. Our conversations, which were always thoughtful, brought us insensibly to a desire for a virtuous love. I was the first to propose a change to Manon. I knew the principles of her heart. She was direct and natural in all her feelings, a quality which always inclines to virtue. I gave her to understand that one thing was lacking to our happiness; it is, said I, to have upon it the approval of Heaven. We both have too fair a soul and too good a heart to live willingly in sin. Enough to have so lived in France, when it was equally impossible for us either to cease to love, or to satisfy ourselves in a legitimate way: but in America, where we depend only upon ourselves, when we no longer need to consider the arbitrary rules of rank and position, where everyone even believes us married, what is to prevent us being so in very truth, and consecrating our love by the vows which Religion ordains? For my own part, I added, I offer you nothing new in offering you my heart and my hand, but I am ready to renew the gift to you at the foot of the Altar. It seemed to me that my words pierced her with joy. Would you believe, she answered, that I have thought about it a thousand times since we came to America? Fear of displeasing made me hide the wish in my heart. I had not the audacity to beg you to give me the right to be your wife. Oh Manon! I replied, you would soon be wife to a King, if Heaven had had me born to a crown. Let us hesitate no longer. We have no obstacle to fear. I am going to speak of it this very day to the Governor, and confess to him that we have been deceiving him until now. Leave it to vulgar lovers, I added, to dread the indissoluble chains of marriage. They would not dread them if they were sure as we are of wearing just as surely those of love. With this resolve I left Manon at the very summit of joy.

I am convinced that there is not an honourable man in the world but would have commended my views in the circumstances as they then stood, myself, that is, fatally enslaved to a passion I could not overcome, and besieged by a remorse I could not stifle. But could one be found to accuse my complaints of injustice, if I bewail the harshness of Heaven in rejecting the design which I had formed to please Him? Alas! do I say, rejecting! it was punished as though it were a crime. He suffered me patiently whilst I walked blindly in the ways of vice, and His sternest chastisements were reserved for me when I began to come back to virtue. I fear I shall lack strength to finish the story of the most mortal blow that ever fell.

I went to the Governor, as I had arranged with Manon, to beg him to consent to the ceremony of our marriage. I should have taken good care to speak of it neither to him nor to anyone if I could have been sure that his Almoner, who was then the sole Priest of the town, would have done me this service without his knowledge: but not daring to hope that he would pledge himself to silence, I judged it better to go about it openly. The Governor had a nephew, one Synnelet, who was very dear to him. He was a man of about thirty, brave, but headstrong and passionate. He was unmarried. The beauty of Manon had stirred him from the moment of our arrival, and the numberless opportunities he had had of seeing her in the last nine or ten months had so inflamed his passion, that he was wearing himself out in secret for her. But as he was convinced, like his uncle and the rest of the town, that I was really married, he had so far mastered his love as to let no spark of it appear and had even shown himself ardent on several occasions to do me a service. On coming into the Fort, I found him with his uncle. I knew no reason to oblige me to keep my intention a secret from him, so that I made no difficulty about explaining myself in his presence. The Governor heard me out with his wonted kindness. I told him part of my story, which he listened to gladly, and when I begged him to be present at the ceremony which I had in mind, he had the generosity to take upon himself all the expenses of the celebration. I withdrew well pleased.

About an hour after, I saw the Almoner enter my house. I imagined that he was coming to give me some instructions as to the wedding, but after greeting me coldly, he informed me in a word or two that his Excellency the Governor forbade me to consider it, and that he had other views for Manon. Other views for Manon! said I, with a deadly clutching at my heart; and what views, pray, Sir Almoner? He answered that I was not unaware that his Excellency the Governor was master; that since Manon had been despatched from France for the Colony, it was his right to dispose of her; that he had not done so until now, believing her already married; but having learned from me that she was not, he thought fit to bestow her upon M. Synnelet, who was in love with her. My quick temper mastered my prudence. I ordered the Almoner haughtily out of my house, swearing that the Governor, Synnelet, and the whole town put together, would not dare to lay a finger on my wife, or my mistress, whatever they chose to call her.

I at once confided in Manon the sinister message I had just received. We concluded that Synnelet had seduced his uncle's mind in the interval, and that it was the outcome of some plot long meditated. They were the stronger. We were set in New Orleans as it were in the midst of the sea, separated from the rest of the world by vast distances. Whither to flee, in an unknown country, deserted, or else inhabited by wild beasts and by Savages as cruel as they? I was respected in the town, but I could not expect so to rouse the people in my favour as to hope for help proportionate to my need. Money would be required; I was poor. Moreover the success of a popular rising was uncertain; and, should fortune fail us, our disaster would be beyond repairing. I turned over all these thoughts in my mind; part of them I shared with Manon; I formed fresh projects without hearing her reply; I took a decision, rejected it to take another; I spoke to myself, replied to my own thoughts aloud; in short, I was in a commotion of spirit that I can compare to nothing, for it had no parallel. Manon's eyes were on me; she judged from my distress the greatness of the peril and, trembling more for me than for herself, the tender creature dared not even open her lips to tell me of her fears. After interminable reflection,

I settled on the resolve to seek out the Governor, and try to move him by considerations of honour and the memory of my respect and his affection. Manon would have prevented my going. Alas! she said to me, weeping: they will kill you: I shall never see you again, unless dead: I want to die before you. It took a good deal of effort to convince her of the necessity of my going out, and of her staying where she was in the house. I promised her that she would see me back in a moment. She did not know, nor did I, that it was upon her the whole wrath of Heaven and the fury of our enemies would fall.

I made my way to the Fort; the Governor was with his Almoner. I humbled myself, to move him, to submission which would have made me die of shame had it been in any other cause: I beset him with whatever considerations could affect a heart less fierce and cruel than a Tiger's. To every appeal the Barbarian made but two replies repeated over and over. Manon, he said, was at his disposal: he had given his word to his nephew. I was resolved to control myself to the last. I contented myself with saying that I thought him too much my friend to will my death, and to that I should consent sooner than to the loss of my mistress.

I was only too well persuaded as I came away that I had nothing to hope for from this obstinate Old Man, who would have seen himself damned a thousand times over for his nephew's sake. I persisted however in my determination to retain to the very last a show of moderation, resolved, if the last outrage of injustice should be done, to give New Orleans one of the bloodiest and most appalling spectacles which love has ever caused. I was on my way home, thinking over my plan, when fate, determined to hasten my ruin, brought Synnelet in my path. He read something of my thought in my eyes. I have said that he was brave: he came up to me. You are looking for me? said he. I know that my designs offend you, and I have foreseen that we should have to cut each other's throats: come, let us see which will be the luckier. I made answer that he was right, and that death alone could put an end to our differences. We took ourselves apart, a hundred yards or so beyond the town. Our swords crossed; I wounded and disarmed him almost at the same moment. He was so infuriated by his ill-luck, that he refused to ask his life from me and give up Manon. I had perhaps a right to deprive him with one thrust of both; but a generous strain does not belie itself. I flung him his sword. Begin again, said I, and remember it is no quarter. He attacked me with unutterable fury. I must confess that I was no great swordsman, having had only three months' fencing in Paris. Love guided my sword. Synnelet succeeded in stabbing me right through the arm, but I took him on the return and gave him a blow so vigorous that he fell motionless at my feet.

In spite of the joy of victory after mortal combat, I saw at once the consequences this death would bring. There would be for me no hope of mercy or delay of execution. Knowing as I did the Governor's passion for his nephew, I was assured that my own death would not be deferred for one hour after his was known. However instant that fear, it was not the gravest cause of my anxiety. Manon, Manon's interest, her peril and the inevitability of her ruin, so troubled me that darkness came before my eyes, and I knew not where I was. I envied Synnelet's fate; a speedy death seemed the only remedy for my sorrows. It was that very thought, however, that recalled me to my senses, and rendered me capable of taking a resolve. What! I would die, I cried, to put an end to my sorrows? And is there one among them I so dread as the loss of my dear Mistress? Ah, suffer whatever must to aid her, and then set about dying when all is suffered in vain! I took the road back to the town. Entering our home, I found Manon half dead with anxiety and dread. My presence revived her. I could not hide from her nor even minimise the terrible accident which had just befallen. On hearing my story of Synnelet's death and my own wound she fell senseless into my arms. It was more than a quarter of an hour before I brought her back to consciousness.

I was half dead myself. I could see no faintest glimmer of hope for her safety or mine. Manon, what shall we do? I asked her, when she had a little recovered. Alas! what are we to do! I must get away. Will you stay in the town? Yes, do you stay here. You can still be happy here, and I shall go, far from you, to seek for death among the Savages, or from the claws of the wild beasts. In spite of her faintness she rose to her feet; she caught my hand to lead me to the door. Let us fly together, she said, and not lose a moment. They may have chanced on Synnelet's body already, and we might not have time to get out of the town. But, dearest Manon, I replied in bewilderment, tell me where we can go? Do you see any refuge? Would it not be better for you to try to live here without me, and I of my own free will offer my head to the Governor? That suggestion only increased her eagerness to be gone. I had to follow her. I had still enough presence of mind, as I went out, to take some strong liquors which I had in the room, and all the provisions that I could cram into my pockets. We said to our Servants who were in the next room that we were going out for our evening stroll (it was our habit every day), and we left the town behind us more quickly than Manon's delicacy might seem to allow.

Although so uncertain as to the goal of our flight, I could see two possibilities, but for which I should have preferred death to uncertainty as to what Manon's fate might be. I had acquired enough knowledge of the country during the ten months that I had been in America, to learn how one might become friendly with the Savages. It was possible to put one's self in their hands without hastening to certain death. I had even learned some words of their language and certain of their customs, on the various opportunities I had had of seeing them. Besides this sorry resource, I had another in the

English, who had, like ourselves, settlements in that part of the New World. But the distance between affrighted me: to reach them we must cross barren plains stretching for several days' journey, and mountains so high and so steep that the path seemed difficult to the hardiest and strongest men. I flattered myself however that we might avail ourselves of both resources; the Savages to help to guide us and the English to receive us into their dwellings.

We walked for as long as Manon's courage could keep her afoot, about two leagues, that is, for this incomparable Lover refused absolutely to halt any sooner. Overwhelmed at last with fatigue, she admitted to me that she could go no further. It was already dark. We sat down in the midst of a vast plain, with not a single tree to give us shelter. Her first care was to change the bandage on my wound, which she had dressed herself before we left. In vain I protested: it would only have been the last blow upon her heart if I had refused her the satisfaction of knowing me comfortable and out of danger, before thinking of her own condition. For some moments I yielded to her wishes. I received her ministrations in silence and with shame, but once she had satisfied her tenderness, with what ardour did not mine take its turn? I stripped myself of my clothes, and put them under her, that she might feel the ground less hard. I made her consent in spite of herself to let me do whatever I could think of to make her less uncomfortable. I warmed her hands by my burning kisses and the warmth of my sighs. I spent the whole night watching beside her, and praying Heaven to give her sweet and quiet sleep. O God! how sincere and eager were my prayers! and by what stern judgment didst Thou resolve to heed them not?

Forgive me if I finish in few words a story that kills me. I have to tell you an illhap that has never had its like. My life is left me now to weep for it. But though I bear it in my memory unceasingly, my soul seems to recoil in horror each time I try to speak of it.

We had passed part of the night in quiet. I thought my dear mistress asleep, and I dared hardly breathe, lest I should disturb her rest. About daybreak, touching her hands, I felt that they were cold and trembling. I brought them to my breast to warm them. She felt the movement, and making an effort to seize my own, she said to me faintly, that she thought she was at her last hour. I only took her words at first as one of the ordinary phrases of misfortune, and only answered by the tender comforting that love inspires. But her frequent sighs, her silence to my questionings, the pressure of her hands which still clung to mine, made me realise that the end of her sorrows was drawing near. Do not ask me to tell you what I felt, nor what were the last words she said to me. I lost her: I had tokens of love from her even as she died; that is all that I have strength to tell you of that fatal and woeful hour.

My soul did not follow hers. Doubtless Heaven judged me not hardly enough punished: He has willed that I should linger out a weary and miserable life. I have no wish that it should ever be happier.

For two days and two nights I stayed, my lips pressed to the face and hands of my dear Manon. I meant to die there: but it came to my mind at the beginning of the third day that her body would be exposed after my death to the ravening of wild beasts. I came to the resolve to bury her, and to wait for death on her grave. I was already so near the end, in the exhaustion due to fasting and sorrow, that I had to make a good many efforts before I could stand. I had to resort to the strong waters which I had brought with me: they gave me what strength was needed for the sorrowful task I must perform. I did not find it hard to open the ground in the spot where I was. The soil was a sandy one. I broke my sword so that I could use it to dig with; but it was less use to me than my own hands. I dug a wide grave. There I laid the idol of my heart, after taking care to wrap all my clothes about her to keep the sand from

"*She felt the movement, and making an effort to seize my own, she said to me faintly, that she thought she was at her last hour*"

touching her. I only laid her so after having kissed her a thousand times with all the passion of a perfect love. I sat there still beside her. I watched her for a long time. I could not bring myself to close her grave. My strength beginning to flag, and fearing that I might fail altogether before I had carried out my task, I buried for ever in the bosom of the earth the loveliest, dearest thing she ever bore. Then I stretched myself upon the grave, my face turned to the sand, and closing my eyes, determined never again to open them, I called on Heaven for succour, and waited impatiently for death. You will find it hard to believe that throughout all the carrying out of that sorrowful task, not a tear fell from my eyes, not a sigh broke from me. My utter disheartening and dismay, my absolute resolve for death, had stopped the channels of despair and grief. And so I was not long laid thus upon the grave before I lost what little of consciousness and feeling remained.

After what you have just heard, the conclusion of my story is so unimportant that it is hardly worth your trouble to listen to it. They brought back Synnelet's body to the town, and once his wounds were carefully searched, he was found to be not only not dead, but not even seriously wounded. He informed his uncle of what had passed between us, and his own generosity made him at once declare frankly what mine had been. I was at once sought for, and my absence with Manon made them suspect that I had decided to take flight. It was too late to follow on my track; but the morrow and the days following were spent in the pursuit. I was found apparently lifeless on Manon's grave, and those who found me, seeing me almost naked and bleeding from my wound, never doubted but that I had been robbed and murdered. They carried me to the town. The motion brought back some consciousness. The sighs which I uttered when on opening my eyes I found myself to my sorrow still among the living, made them realise that I was still within reach of aid: it was given, too successfully. On my arrival, I did not fail to be shut up in close confinement. The charge against me was drawn up, and as Manon did not appear, I was accused of having made away with her in a fit of rage and jealousy. I told them simply the pitiable story. Synnelet, despite the agonies of grief into which it threw him, had the generosity to entreat my pardon. It was granted him. I was so weak that I had to be carried from prison in my bed, and there I lay for three months, dangerously ill. My hatred of life did not lessen. I ceased not to call on death, and for a long time I persisted in rejecting all remedies; but Heaven, after pursuing me with so much sternness, had planned my sorrows and His chastisements to my profit. The light of His grace fell on me, and He inspired in me the resolve to return to Him by the road of penitence. Peace at last having begun to dawn in my soul, the change in me was closely followed by my recovery. I gave my whole heart to the exercises of religion, and I continued to discharge my minor office, in expectation of the ships from France, which come once a year to that part of America. I had resolved to return to my native land, to make amends by a wise and ordered life for the scandal of my past conduct. I saw to it that the body of my dear mistress should be brought to holy ground. It was not long after this that walking one day alone by the shore, I saw the arrival of a ship which called to trade at New Orleans. I stood watching the disembarking of its passengers, when I was struck with the utmost astonishment at seeing Tiberge among those making their way to the town. This faithful friend recognised me a great way off in spite of the changes which grief had wrought in my countenance. He told me that the only motive of his journey had been the wish to see me and persuade me to return to France: after receiving the letter I had written him from Havre, he had come there in person to bring me the help I begged for: that he had felt the sharpest pain on hearing of my departure, and would have set out there and then to follow me if he had found a ship ready to sail: that he had sought for months through several ports, and at last finding one in St. Malo about to sail for Quebec, he had gone on board, hoping to find an easy passage thence to New Orleans: that the Malouin vessel having been captured at sea by Spanish Pirates, and taken to one of their Islands, he had escaped by a trick, and after various journeys, had chanced on the vessel which had just arrived, to reach me happily at last.

I could not sufficiently show my gratitude for so constant and so generous a friend. I brought him to my house. I made him master of all I had. I told him all that had befallen me since my departure from France: and to give him a joy beyond his expectation, I told him that the seeds of goodness which he had once sown in my heart were beginning at last to bring forth fruits that might content him. He declared that such tidings recompensed him fully for all the fatigues of his voyage.

We spent two months together at New Orleans, awaiting the arrival of the ships from France, and, putting at last to sea, we landed a fortnight ago at Havre-de-Grâce. I wrote to my family on my arrival. I have learned, from my elder brother's reply, the sad news of the death of my father. The wind being favourable for Calais, I embarked at once, with the intention of coming to this town to the house of a Gentleman of my own kin, where my brother writes that he will await my arrival.

APPENDIX

THE episode of the Italian prince was inserted by the Abbé Prévost in the edition of 1753, 'for the plenitude of one of the principal characters.' In the original, the sound of the carriage is heard while Manon and M. de T . . . and the Chevalier are still at their joyous supper. Here, that supper is only the first of many, and weeks elapse before young G . . . M . . . makes his fatal entrance. The episode begins a new paragraph, after the one ending 'and that it seemed I could not fail of, either from my family or from the gaming table' on p. 85.·

"THUS, for the first few weeks, I had no thought but to enjoy my situation: my sense of honour, and some remnant of discretion as regarded the Police, made me put off from day to day renewing relations with the Fraternity at the Hôtel de Transylvanie, and I confined play to various less notorious Assemblies, where the favours of Fortune spared me the humiliation of having recourse to manipulation. I used to spend part of the afternoon in Town, coming back to sup at Chaillot, very often accompanied by M. de T . . ., whose friendship with us grew from day to day. Manon found resources against boredom. She made friends in the neighbourhood with a few young people whom Spring had brought to the country; walking and the trifling employments of their sex kept them occupied in turn. A game of cards, in which they limited the stakes, would pay for the cost of the carriage. They would go to take the air in the Bois de Boulogne, and in the evening, on my return, I would find Manon lovelier, more contented, and more passionate than ever.

There were, it is true, some clouds that rose to threaten my happiness. But they soon were dissolved into clear air, and Manon's madcap humour made the climax so comical that I find sweetness even yet in a memory that brings back to me her tenderness and the delight of her wit.

The single Manservant who represented our household took me one day aside to tell me with a good deal of embarrassment that he had an important secret to tell me. I encouraged him to speak freely. After some beating about the bush, he let me know that a Foreign Nobleman seemed to have fallen very much in love with Mademoiselle Manon. I was sensible of the stirring of my blood through every vein. Has she fallen in love with him? I broke in, more brusquely than was prudent, if I wished for enlightenment. My quickness terrified him. He answered with an uneasy look that he could not say he had seen anything of that; but that he had noticed for several days that this Foreigner came punctiliously to the Bois de Boulogne, that he would leave his coach, and wander about by himself in the side-alleys, seemingly on the watch for an opportunity to see or meet Mademoiselle, and so it had occurred to my man to strike up acquaintance with the other's servants so as to learn their master's name: that they spoke of him as an Italian Prince, and themselves suspected there was some gallantry afoot: he had not been able to get any more hints, he added, trembling, because the prince at that moment came out of the Bois, came towards him in friendly fashion, and asked him his name; after which, as though divining him to be in our service, he congratulated him on belonging to the most charming Person in the world.

I waited impatiently for the end of his tale. He wound up by timid excuses, which I put down to my own imprudence in showing my agitation. In vain I pressed him to go on, dissembling nothing. He protested that he knew nothing more, and that as what he had just told me had happened only the day before, he had not seen the Prince's people again. I reassured him, not only by praising him, but with a respectable reward; and without showing the least mistrust of Manon, I bade him, in a lighter tone, to keep watch on all the Foreigner's movements.

At bottom, his alarm left me miserably ill at ease. I felt that it had made him suppress part of the truth. However, after thinking it over, I shook off my fears so far as to regret having shown any signs of weakness. I could not make it a crime in Manon that she was loved. There was much to suggest that she was unaware of her Conquest; and what kind of life was I going to lead, if I could so readily admit jealousy into my heart? I went back to Paris next day, without having formed any further plan than to hasten the building up of my fortune by playing for higher stakes, so as to be able to leave Chaillot at the first suggestion of alarm. That evening I heard nothing to disturb my rest. The Foreigner had appeared in the Bois de Boulogne, and presuming on what had passed the previous day to get on terms with my Informant, he had spoken to him of his love, but in a fashion that implied no understanding with Manon. He had questioned him on a thousand points. Finally he had tried to win him to his interests by large promises, and drawing out a letter which he had ready, he had offered him several louis d'or to take it to his Mistress, but in vain.

Two days passed without any further incident. The third was more stormy. Coming back rather late from town, I learned that Manon, during the walk, had strayed for a moment from her Companions, and that the Foreigner, who was following her a little way off, came up to her at a sign she made him, and she had then given him a letter, which he took with transports of joy. He had only time to express them by amorous kisses on the handwriting, because she had at once slipped away. But she had seemed in extraordinary spirits for the rest of the day; and her gaiety had not subsided since she had come home. I shuddered at every word. Are you quite sure, said I sadly to my Valet, that your eyes have not deceived you? He took Heaven to witness to his good faith. I do not know whither the torment of my heart might not have hurried me, had not Manon, on hearing me come in, come to meet me all impatience and complaints of my slowness. She did not wait for my reply to smother me with caresses: and as soon as she was alone with me, she began to reproach me very vigorously for the habit I was falling into of coming home so late. My silence left her free to continue, and she told me that for three weeks I had not spent one whole day with her: that she could not bear such long absences: that she would demand at least one day every now and then, and that to-morrow she wanted to see me beside her from morning till night. I shall be there, depend on it, I answered, shortly enough. She paid small attention to my annoyance, and in high glee, for she seemed to me unusually gay, made me a score of jesting sketches of how she had spent the day. Strange Girl, said I to myself, what am I to expect from this prelude? The thought of what had happened before our first separation came back to me. Yet behind all her gaiety and her caresses I thought I perceived a sincerity that matched the outward seeming.

My dejection persisted throughout supper: I could not shake it off, but threw the blame for it on a loss I complained of at Cards. I was heartily pleased that the suggestion about my not leaving Chaillot next day had come from herself. It gave me more time to think things over. My being there banished all fears for the morrow: and if I saw nothing that would force me to blazon my discoveries, I was already determined to transfer my household the day after to Town, to some quarter where I need not have to do with Princes. The thought of this arrangement helped me to a tranquil night: but it could not do away with the pain of having to tremble for a fresh infidelity.

Once awake, Manon vowed that even if I were going to spend the day in our apartment, she would not have me any less spick and span, and she would even dress my hair with her own hands. My hair used to be handsome enough, and she sometimes amused herself dressing it. But she now took more pains with it than I had ever known her do before. To satisfy her, I was obliged to sit down in front of her dressing-table, and submit to all the devices she could think of for my adornment. In the course of her work she would often make me turn my face towards her, and, resting both hands on my shoulders, she would gaze at me with eager curiosity; then, showing her satisfaction by a kiss or two, she would have me take up my old position while she went on with her task. This pretty nonsense kept us busy till dinner time. The pleasure she was finding in it had so natural an air, and her gaiety so little of artifice that I could not reconcile such appearance of devotion with the project of black treachery, and was tempted more than once to open my heart to her, and unburden it of a load that was beginning to weigh heavy on me. But I flattered myself every moment that the first word would come from her, and promised myself beforehand a delicious triumph.

We came back into our study. She began to rearrange my hair, and I was indulgently submitting to all her whims, when the servant announced that the Prince de ... was asking to see her. The name kindled me to fury. What? I exclaimed, pushing her away. Who? What Prince? She made no answer to my questions. Bring him up, said she coldly to our Man; and turning to me, Dear Love, said she, and her voice was enchantment, I ask you, you whom I worship, to indulge me a moment. One moment. One single moment. I shall love you a thousand times more for it. I shall be grateful to you all my life.

Indignation and surprise kept me tongue-tied. She continued her entreaties, and I sought for words that would repel them with scorn. But leaving the door of the ante-room open, with one hand she caught hold of my hair which was flowing over my shoulders, took up her mirror in the other, threw all her strength into dragging me in that guise to the door of the study, opened it with her knee, and presented to the Stranger, halted by the commotion in the middle of the room, a spectacle which must have caused him no little amazement. I saw a man elegantly dressed, but somewhat ill-favoured. In spite of his embarrassment, he did not fail to make a profound bow. Manon did not give him time to open his mouth. She held up her mirror before him. Come, Sir, said she, take a good look at yourself and do me justice. You ask me for my love. Here is the man I love, and whom I have sworn to love all my life. Do you yourself make the comparison. If you think you can dispute my heart with him, tell me on what grounds: for I declare to you that in the eyes of your very humble Servant, all the Princes in Italy are not worth one of these locks that I hold.

Throughout this mad speech which she had evidently prepared, I was making useless efforts to get free; and taking pity on a man of some distinction, I felt myself called on to atone for this petty outrage by my courtesy. But his recovery was swift, and my mood changed on hearing the touch of coarseness in his reply. Mademoiselle, mademoiselle, said he, forcing a smile, I do indeed open my eyes, and find you considerably less of the Novice than I had imagined. He withdrew without another glance at her, adding in an undertone that the Women of France were worth no more than those of Italy. I was not impelled, on that occasion, to urge him to a juster view of the fair Sex.

Manon let go my hair, threw herself into an armchair, and made the room ring with continued bursts of laughter. I do not pretend that I was not touched to the heart by a sacrifice that I could only attribute to Love. None the less the jest seemed to me to have been carried too far, and I reproached her for it. She told me that my Rival, after dogging her steps for some days in the Bois, and endeavouring to convey his sentiments by his grimaces, had finally made up his mind to make a formal declaration, accompanied by his name and all his titles, in a Letter which he had given her by the Coachman who drove her and her Companions; that he promised her a brilliant future and eternal adoration, beyond the Mountains; that she had come back to Chaillot intending to tell me of her adventure, but once the thought struck her that we might get some merriment out of it, she could not resist it; that she had sent a flattering Reply to the Italian Prince, giving him permission to come and see her, and that she had found fresh delight in bringing me into her scheme, without letting me have the faintest suspicion of it. I did not tell her a word of the light I had had upon it from another quarter, and the intoxication of triumphant Love made me approve it all."

[The original narrative now continues, with the necessary verbal alterations. 'I thought myself so happy, supping with M. de T . . . and Manon,' becomes 'I thought myself so happy with the friendship of M. de T . . ., and Manon's tenderness.' 'Whilst we were at table' becomes 'One day that we had M. de T . . . to supper, we heard the sound of a carriage stopping at the door of the inn.']

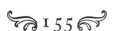